Erin was awa...
felt liberating...
so, to just loo...
appreciate him. It felt good to not
be taken, spoken for, committed.

Snow blew in, right up under the porch. When she stepped back, Valentino had not moved but was studying the interior of the cabin. The look on his face was extraordinary. It was as if he was lit from within. Her eyes moved to the puffiness of that lower lip again.

Then he threw back his head and laughed. *"Encantado,"* he declared softly, his accent unconsciously seductive. And then his eyes came to rest on her. He had spoken in Spanish, so he translated. "I'm enchanted."

She felt as if her breath stopped.

Was he referring to her? To her gazing at his lips? She was shocked to feel something primitive and powerful stir within her. After all, she knew nothing about this man who was looking so intently at her with a gaze that set fire in her blood. *Wanting.*

Wanting what? Erin asked herself primly. She just wasn't the kind of girl who went around lusting after strangers on the ski hill.

She sighed inwardly. The universe had not only provided her with a Valentino for Valentine's Day, but one that was going to challenge everything she believed about herself.

Dear Reader,

This morning I came across a story I must have written very shortly after learning to print. It was called *Mary May and the Goldfish*, and it reminded me I've really never been "in" the world.

Looking back, I was probably the weird one. While everyone else walked to school, I rode the prancing horses of a fertile imagination. I didn't play in the backyard; I was a tightrope walker at the circus. I *always* had a story on the go, and I was always more immersed in that than in what was really going on around me.

To this day, I absolutely love the world of my imagination. All these years later, I can't believe my luck that I get to share that world—imaginary kingdoms, a handsome prince, an ordinary girl finding magic—with you.

Thank you for allowing me to have a life beyond anything I could have ever imagined for myself.

With heartfelt gratitude to each of you,

Cara Colter

Snowbound with the Prince

Cara Colter

—

HARLEQUIN®

Romance™

Recycling programs
for this product may
not exist in your area.

ISBN-13: 978-1-335-40692-7

Snowbound with the Prince

Copyright © 2021 by Cara Colter

This edition published by arrangement with Harlequin Books S.A.

For questions and comments about the quality of this book,
please contact us at CustomerService@Harlequin.com.

Harlequin Enterprises ULC
22 Adelaide St. West, 41st Floor
Toronto, Ontario M5H 4E3, Canada
www.Harlequin.com

Printed in U.S.A.

Cara Colter shares her life in beautiful British Columbia, Canada, with her husband, nine horses and one small Pomeranian with a large attitude. She loves to hear from readers, and you can learn more about her and contact her through Facebook.

Books by Cara Colter

Harlequin Romance

A Fairytale Summer!

Cinderella's New York Fling

Cinderellas in the Palace

His Convenient Royal Bride
One Night with Her Brooding Bodyguard

A Crown by Christmas

Cinderella's Prince Under the Mistletoe

Matchmaker and the Manhattan Millionaire
His Cinderella Next Door
The Wedding Planner's Christmas Wish

Visit the Author Profile page
at Harlequin.com for more titles.

To all those kindred spirits who have found sanctuary and salvation through imagination.

Praise for
Cara Colter

"Ms. Colter's writing style is one you will want to continue to read. Her descriptions place you there.... This story does have a HEA but leaves you wanting more."

—*Harlequin Junkie* on *His Convenient Royal Bride*

CHAPTER ONE

VALENTINE'S DAY TOMORROW.

Was there a worse day to be single? Particularly newly single? Somehow, Erin O'Rourke had thought Valentine's Day, this year, was going to be extra special.

After the disappointment of no ring at Christmas, she thought Paul had decided on the much more romantic Valentine's Day to spring the question.

Erin had pictured wine. Roses. And maybe, just maybe, a ring, small diamonds sparkling, tucked into the red velvet petals of one of those roses.

But she couldn't have been more wrong. How could she have missed all the signals? How could she have interpreted a situation so incorrectly?

Two weeks ago, Paul had announced, *It just isn't working.*

Erin had been stunned. It wasn't?

While she was indulging a fantasy of commitment—wedded bliss; a little house; someday soon, a baby—her boyfriend of two years, Paul, had been moving in the opposite direction. How to get out of it. How to escape the traditional values—the ones she had adored—of the family he had been raised in.

So, instead of celebrating her new engagement, here Erin was on the eve of Valentine's Day. Free. Well, basically free. There was always, thank goodness, Harvey.

She patted the bulge of precious cargo at her tummy, pulled her toque down even lower over her brow and her ears, her hair all tucked beneath it.

She had just gotten off the Lonesome Lookout chairlift, the highest chair at Touch-the-Clouds ski resort. Her grandfather had started the Rocky Mountain resort more than fifty years ago.

The resort had come a long way from its humble beginnings. It had once had a single chairlift and a T-bar, a simple, cavernous lodge heated by a stove made from a salvaged oil barrel.

But Touch-the-Clouds had some of the best deep powder in the world and, over the years, it was a secret that had gotten out. It had grown in popularity, particularly with the rich and famous. Finally, it had grown beyond her grandfather's capacity to keep up.

It now consisted of an entire village with bars and hotels, shops, restaurants and condos. It offered a dozen different chairlifts and hundreds of runs. While it was still the preferred ski retreat of the rich and famous, everything depended on snow. They'd had a bad few years.

And a bad review in *Snow Lust* magazine. The resort had been called "tired and overrated."

Although it was owned by a big corporation now—as were most high-end ski resorts that wanted to be viable—Erin was employed in the accounting department, and she knew the resort had spent several years in the red. How long could they keep that up? She lived at an apartment provided for her in the ski village complex, and she still had exclusive use of her grandfather's original cabin, Snow Daze, but for how long? The cabin was well off the beaten track, and the snowy trail to it could only be accessed from this chairlift.

She had decided that Snow Daze was where she would spend Valentine's Day, taking the day off tucked away in the rustic cabin. She hoped the intense quiet of deep snow outside and the crackle of a fire inside, and a cat on her lap, would soothe something in her, as they always had.

That way, tomorrow, she would not be on the receiving end of sympathetic looks from her coworker, Kelly, as she acted surprised and gleeful over the delivery of flowers and a gooey card from her husband.

Erin had, so far, managed to keep her humiliating breakup to herself.

See? There was a good side to Paul never producing a ring. A suddenly naked ring finger was like sending out an announcement card.

However, so was *nothing* arriving for her at the office on February fourteenth. It would be the equivalent of posting a group email around the office, its message the opposite of a valentine. *I'm a failure at love. It didn't work. I'm single.*

Erin regarded the mountain in the waning light of a cold winter day. She knew it as few people did, and the snow was now coming so thick and fast that she could no longer see the peaks of the mountains that surrounded this bowl.

She had caught the chair as the old attendant, Ricky, was turning everyone else away for the day.

"You're cutting it close," he'd warned her.

"I sent the ski patrol up twenty minutes ago to sweep the mountain for stragglers. You're only about thirty minutes from full dark. I don't think you can make it all the way down in that time."

"I'm not going all the way down. I'm heading to the cabin," she'd said. "Lots of time for that." She'd patted her front pocket. "I've got a satellite device. I'll let the patrol know when I get there."

He'd cast a look at the thickly falling flakes of snow. "Okay, but be careful."

She had actually laughed. "Going to that cabin for me is as routine as an afternoon commute for most people."

"I know," he'd said. "I helped your grandpa build that place. I know you're as at home here as anywhere else. But it's still a mountain, and Mother Nature can still surprise you. That looks like one doozy of a storm building. I don't think we could mount a rescue in it."

"You won't be rescuing me," she had assured him.

His concern for her had been a comfort.

On the chair, she put a hand on the warmth radiating from her belly and said out loud, "*This* is our family. Touch-the-Clouds is our home."

And that, Erin was determined, would be enough.

Now, at the top of the run, in absolute solitude, Erin pulled her hood up as extra protection from the heavily falling snow, and slid her goggles over her eyes. She used her poles to shove off and heard the wonderful hiss of her ski edges cutting into the new powder.

She crouched, picked up momentum and speed, and felt her heartaches blow away as she became fully immersed in the exhilaration of the moment.

Snow, wind, the skis beneath her. Since she was a child, those things had filled her heart with a euphoria that nothing else had ever replicated.

Including her love for Paul, she realized.

She had also been going to Snow Daze since she was a baby. Her memories of the cabin were of multigenerational family gatherings. She had grown up to ducking through strings of clothes drying by the fire, wet from sledding and building snowmen. Her memories were hot-chocolate scented, rambunctious card games won and lost around a beat-up wooden table, books devoured in a rump-sprung easy chair, waxing skis on the kitchen counter.

Still, realistically, hadn't those moments

been few and far between? Her father's pro racing, and then his coaching career, had sent him all over the world. Her mother, exhausted from his inability to say no to anyone who was charmed by the combination of fame and extraordinarily good looks, had finally left him when Erin was eleven.

The remainder of her childhood had been spent between their two households, with their ever-changing international backdrops. And partners.

She had longed for the things other people's families stood for and that they seemed to take for granted.

Stability. Connection. Loyalty. Love.

Those were the things she had hoped for when she'd started dating Paul… Erin shook it off. The entrance to the trail that led to the cabin was difficult to find at the best of times. Part of the healing power of the mountain was that it forced you to stay focused.

There was no room up here for daydreaming. There were consequences for errors. It would be too easy in these conditions, even for someone as familiar with the mountain as she was, to swoop by the trailhead and have to do the arduous, sidestepping climb to backtrack up to it in the growing dark and the thickening storm.

She skidded to a halt, loving the wave of snow that shot out from her skis, the familiar ache of muscles used hard. Between wind gusts, it was deeply silent. Even the rumbling hum of the chairlift was gone, shut off for the day.

Still, the snowfall, she realized, was developing a different quality, becoming shardlike. She squinted through ice-crusted goggles up the hill and then slid them onto her forehead. She caught a single glimpse of the sky. It was taking on the ominous purplish tint that said, to those who knew the mountain, a storm was coming.

A doozy of a storm, just as Ricky had predicted.

She might end up at the cabin for more than a day, but that suited her. The cabin was always well stocked, plus she had, in her backpack, a special Valentine's feast for one. She could check in with the resort by her sat device to let them know her plans.

Paul, not much of a skier, had never been to the cabin, so there was nothing there to remind her of him.

Had she deliberately saved it? Thinking it would be the most delightful place in the world for a honeymoon? Thinking, if they had a summer wedding, they could hike into that secluded place, untouched by modern technologies, and have a few blissful days all to themselves?

No phones. No computers. No interruptions.

Paul and his phone: the constant checking, tapping away, shutting out the world, shutting out her...

Again, she shook off her sudden awareness of the insult of it. Instead, Erin looked toward the tree line. Barely visible was the tiny opening that marked a secret trail. Nailed above it was a small sign, faded, nearly covered with snow, that said Private. No Entrance. It was a largely unnecessary warning since only someone looking for this narrow gap in the wall of silent, snow-covered fir could find it.

She slid the goggles back down, tightened her hood, and pointed her skis toward the opening. She was just about to plant her poles when a voice stopped her. Was it a voice? Or just the storm announcing it was intensifying with the odd howling wind gust?

She had thought she was alone on the mountain. She turned and squinted up into the driving snow. She saw nothing.

But then she heard the voice, louder than before. Definitely not the wind.

"Alisha, wait." The voice was deep and masculine.

Alisha? Did that mean there were two people still out on the slopes in the storm? She couldn't see anyone, the snow was so thick. Erin noticed it was beginning to blow sideways rather than drift straight down.

Then the veil of snow lifted and she saw him, making his way down the mountain toward her. It was a steep section and the visibility had gone extraordinarily flat, but he was a good skier, very technical, and she could see a natural athleticism in the aggressive way he tackled the challenging slope and traversed the ground between them.

He swooshed to a stop in front of her, covering her in a cascading wave of snow as powdery as icing sugar. As she shook it off, she was irritated, not because he had covered her with snow, but because he was still on the mountain after it had been swept.

Still, her annoyance abated somewhat as she became aware of his sheer physical presence. The storm seemed to pause around them. The wind and snow stopped abruptly. Was it possible it was going to blow over? Not likely.

He was much taller than she was and for some reason she noted that, probably because for two years she had been trying to shrink, as if her being taller than him was some sort of slight to Paul.

The athleticism she had seen in the way this man navigated the hill was even more apparent at close range. His shoulders were broad under a very expensive ski jacket and he wore the tight, flexible pant of a ski racer. Those pants molded the large muscles of powerful thighs. He carried himself with such sheer confidence that the reprimand she wanted to give him—what the heck was he still doing on the mountain—died before she spoke it.

It felt as if he, not she, had been born to this mountain, as if he owned not just it, but all the earth.

His eyes were covered by mirrored goggles. Below those goggles, he had chosen to be unprotected from the conditions by not pulling his neck gaiter up over his face. Was there something vaguely familiar about him? Probably. She had likely seen him around the resort village. He was the kind of man you would notice—and then quickly *not* notice— if you had recently been devastated by a long-term relationship exploding in your face.

Or fizzling, as the case might be.

She had to ground herself. She could not let the lull in the storm distract her from the seriousness of his situation, or that of his still missing companion, Alisha.

But instead of feeling grounded, Erin felt compelled to look at him again. A renegade tingle went up and down her spine.

It was just the wild unpredictability of the winter weather, Erin assured herself. It was increasing the intensity of her awareness of everything, including the stranger who had come out of its understated prelude.

Coming storms did this, infused the air and the earth with a humming current, both powerful and mystic. The awareness she was feeling because of the storm was transferring to him, it wasn't *because* of him.

If she thought about it, she was also aware of the feeling of each snowflake falling on her face, the deep, muffled quiet, the scent that always rode in with strong weather. Indefinable. Pure. Untamed.

"Alisha," he said. "I thought I had lost you."

Any illusion Erin had that the intensity of her awareness was caused by the mountain preparing to unleash its savagery around them evaporated.

His voice was like warm honey. It was deeply and deliciously exotic. He had the faintest accent that carried her far away from the storm, to sun-drenched places that smelled of spice and flowers.

She wished she was Alisha.

Slowly, with a sigh, she lifted her hand, flipped down her hood and then raised her goggles off her eyes.

CHAPTER TWO

PRINCE VALENTINO DE OSCARO STARED, shocked, into the greenest eyes he had ever seen. The shock was intensified because he thought he had finally, in this lull in the snowstorm that was in equal parts terrifying and exhilarating, been reunited with his head of security.

"You're not Alisha," he said.

It was stating the obvious. The ski jackets, the height—unusually tall for a woman—were similar enough that he had made the initial error of thinking it was Alisha, particularly since that was who he had been looking for. What were the chances, after all, of two women of similar appearance being out in this storm?

But his head of security, Colonel Alisha Del Rento, was the antithesis of this woman: her life experiences honed into her face, unapologetically tough and weathered. The colonel was as dark as this woman was pale.

The prince realized the word *pale* did not do justice to the woman in front of him. *Fair* might be better. There was the wholesome glow of the outdoors dusted on her skin, giving her a look most women would want but that could never be attained out of a makeup bottle.

These observations were peripheral. Where was Alisha? Though she took pride in the fact that she could handle anything that life threw at her, neither she nor the other two members of his security team were familiar with this mountain.

They had, he knew, trained for winter conditions, but still he felt concerned. This was on him. He had insisted, despite the worsening weather and against his security team's wishes, on one more run, the new snow making the powder too exquisite to resist.

The woman might not physically resemble the colonel in any way, but that tight-lipped look of disapproval was familiar.

"What on earth are you doing out here?" the woman asked.

Valentino was unaccustomed to sharpness of tone and, despite his worry for his team, he felt oddly delighted by it.

Just as he felt oddly delighted by the storm. It was so real. A man and a mountain, pitting his strength, his abilities, his intelligence, against the elements.

Of course, he had two women, now, who were really annoyed at him. The one before him, whose green eyes were sparking with an intriguing inner light, and his head of security, who had strongly advised, given the weather, they not make this final run.

But he had insisted, *loving* the challenge of it.

Only one of those women would feel free to express her chagrin, and that was the one in front of him.

He felt himself rising to the challenge of her, too. He answered her question by repeating it.

"What on earth are *you* doing out here?" he shot back.

Her look of disapproval intensified. Who, besides his mother, had ever dared be disapproving of him?

"I live here."

He glanced around. "Where? Under one of the trees?"

She failed, apparently, to see the humor. "I also work here. You shouldn't be on the mountain in this storm."

"But you should?" he asked mildly. "Besides, it seems to be letting up."

"I thought so, too, but don't underestimate mountain weather. It's possible it has barely hit yet."

Could that be true? The snow had paused but was coming again, though lighter than it had been before. The wind had died down almost completely.

Glaring at him, as if he was a horrible inconvenience to her, she planted her poles and pulled off her gloves. He was not sure why he noticed her fingers were ringless. She unzipped an outer pocket of her jacket. He noticed a slight bump at her waistline and something in him went cold.

Was she pregnant?

Valentino felt suddenly and astonishingly protective of her—and also in way over his head. As he looked at her, the bulge in her stomach area *moved*.

Good grief, was she going to have a baby? Out here in a storm that, according to her, had barely hit yet? With him, of all people? He wasn't wholly loving the challenge of the mountain—and of her—quite so much now.

Thankfully, she produced a cumbersome item that looked like some kind of phone, and he felt the relief sigh within him. Signals on his own cell phone had been intermittent since arriving at the resort.

She held her apparatus up to the sky and shifted her glare from him to it. She took a few sidesteps up the mountain, and he recognized, despite her condition, how at ease she was on the skis.

She held up the device again.

"What are you doing?" he asked.

"Searching for a signal. It's a satellite device," she said without looking at him. Her face brightened. She quickly lowered the device, punched in numbers, and put it to her ear.

"What's your name?"

Valentino simply was not accustomed to being snapped at like this: as if he were some sort of nuisance, causing aggravation to someone. Despite the fact that he was somewhat lost, with a storm apparently nowhere near over, with a woman who was pregnant, he contemplated how what should have been an insult instead felt oddly refreshing.

Had he ever, in his entire life, had someone have absolutely no idea of who he was?

And so, he didn't want her to know. Not just yet. He would enjoy this anonymity for a little while longer by just giving his first name. Of course, once she got someone on the other end of that phone, she was bound to find out the Crown Prince of the Kingdom of Lorenzo del Toro was missing.

"Valentino," he said. He wanted to say something more North American. Like Fred. Or Joe. But there was the security team to consider. They would be frantic with worry for him, wherever they were. So, as delightful as it would be to remain anonymous, his duty to others came first. As always.

"Seriously?" Her green eyes narrowed skeptically on him, as if he *had* given her a pseudonym.

"Excuse me?"

"Your name is Valentino?"

"It is," he said.

"What are the chances?" she muttered.

"Excuse me?" he said again.

She sighed heavily. "What are the chances that I would find a man named Valentino on the mountain on the eve of Valentine's Day?"

"It had completely slipped my mind that tomorrow is Valentine's Day," he told her. Then, before he could ask her name in return—and if she shouldn't be with her husband to have her baby on Valentine's Day—she moved on, snapping another question at him.

"And your companion? Alisha? When's the last time you saw her?"

"We were on the chair together. There were actually four of us total."

"Four?" she said, and her green eyes widened in alarm. Now was probably not the time to notice how thick her lashes were, the snowflakes—the snow *was* deepening again—crusting on them like tiny diamonds.

It might reduce her alarm to tell her his team were all specialists in a number of areas that would likely more than prepare them for the challenges of the mountain. But then, he was concerned about them himself, and admitting to being accompanied by a "team" of specialists of any kind would certainly give clues that she had not run into just an ordinary joe on the mountain.

The prince was not yet ready to give up his taste of anonymity.

"Yes, we were skiing together. They're very accomplished."

Her look of skepticism was not reduced. Again, it was novel to have someone doubt him.

"To be honest," he offered, "I don't know how we were separated. It seems impossible."

Given his team's absolute devotion to his protection and safety, it really did seem astonishing that somehow they had lost each other. One moment he had been swooping down the mountain, elated, and the next he had been aware of the deepening of the storm and that he was alone.

"The mountains love to make fun of what people think is possible and impossible," she said and then turned her attention to the phone.

"Hi, Stacy. This is Erin."

Erin. He contemplated that name and how well it suited her. In his world, women had feminine names, so this added to his sense of being let loose in a different time and place.

Erin's voice drifted to him. For all that her name wasn't particularly feminine, her voice was.

"I've come across a guy up here on the Lonesome runs. Valentino."

He was irrationally glad he hadn't told her he was Joe or Fred, because he liked the way his name sounded coming off her lips.

"Four total in his party," she said then raised her voice. "Four."

She listened and then pulled the phone away from her ear. Even with a bit of distance between them, he could hear a hissing and crackling on the line. She waited, patiently, until it subsided, and put the device back up to her ear.

He expected his moment of anonymity was

about to be lost. She would be told she was with a member of the royal family from a small Mediterranean island kingdom. Everything would change. She would look at him with deference, a new respect, but it would be because of his title, not because of who he was. He felt unreasonably deflated by that.

She was squinting at her device, disgruntled. She held it up, sighed, then shoved it back in her pocket.

"The signal evaporated," she said with a shrug, none the wiser to who he was. "Which is not so surprising in this weather. But I understand that the rest of your party is accounted for, thank goodness."

His sense of relief was instant. Despite the fact the soldiers of his personal guard were experts who had trained in survival from the Italian Alps to the Arctic Ocean, he still had known it was because of him they'd been out in the storm. If anything had happened...

"Good," he said. "I'll meet them down there."

She looked pensively at the weather, took in a deep breath of the air, as if it gave her clues.

"We aren't going down," she decreed.

We? And who had placed *her* in charge of

him? He raised an eyebrow. In his world, that was all it took.

But she knew nothing of his world.

"I think it's too close to dark," she stated. "We can't make it all the way down to the village, especially if the storm gets worse, which I think it is going to."

"Do we have an option?" he asked. He did not want to be trapped on a mountain, in a storm, with a woman who looked like she might be about to have a baby. His gaze drifted to the terrifying bump at her belly. He thought he detected a slight motion again. A baby at any moment!

Again, she considered the weather. "I don't think so."

"What exactly does that mean?" Valentino asked. "That we have to shelter up here?" He had kidded her about living under one of the trees, but now it didn't seem funny.

She was silent and preoccupied, pulling the goggles back over her eyes, fastening her hood tight around her toque.

"We can build an igloo," he proposed. He couldn't have predicted that this morning. That he would be building a shelter, a storm raging, a baby coming. His life rarely handed him surprises. But he didn't feel trepidation about the challenge.

Instead, he felt ready. Protective. And fierce, as if a warrior spirit he had not known he'd possessed had stepped up to do battle with these elements.

He felt the huge weight of the responsibility to get her through this, but he also felt ready to test himself against the mountain, to not be pampered and protected. But instead to be the protector. He felt astonishingly alive, vibrating with urgency.

"An igloo?"

He frowned at her. The one who claimed to live here didn't seem to be getting the peril they were in since she had decided they couldn't make it back to the village. It was probably a form of protective denial. Because of the baby.

"Yes, you know," he said, keeping his voice calm, patient, reassuring. "We'll have to find some crusted snow. And cut blocks from it. It will protect us from the elements until morning."

"I know what an igloo is." For the first time, a smile tickled her lips. He noticed they were unglossed and generous. And gorgeous.

What kind of man made that kind of note about a pregnant woman's lips? It seemed like something you might have to admit to in the confessional!

Besides, he had to keep the priorities straight, since she was obviously not going to. How could she not know how dangerous this all could become in the blink of an eye?

Still, that smile changed everything about her. The sternness left her face and she looked very youthful and wholesome, not to mention extraordinarily beautiful.

And then she laughed.

He might have enjoyed the sound of that more if he hadn't had the annoying sense she was not just making light of their predicament, but laughing *at* him. Not *with him*— because he was not laughing.

This was an extraordinarily novel experience. Not at all enjoyable, like his anonymity had been.

"An igloo," she snorted between chortles.

He frowned at her. Was she mocking him? A frown from him had always been enough to bring instant respect. She, however, did not take the frown as a reprimand, as he had intended. Not at all.

"And you know how to make one?" she asked, the music of her laughter still tinging her voice. "An igloo? Or do you think I know how to make one? A mandatory part of being Canadian?"

She was continuing to be amused at his expense! The novelty of her not knowing who he was, was thinning rapidly.

"I'm sure I can figure it out," he informed her stiffly. "I saw it on a documentary once."

She managed to contain, finally, her awful chortling, though her lips still twitched. "Well, that would certainly make you an expert," she said. Her tone was not sarcastic, but soothing, which made it twice as insulting, as if she were speaking to a child who had told her he knew how to build a rocket ship to the moon.

"I could, in a pinch, put together a rudimentary shelter from the elements."

"Yes, of course, you could." There was the patronizing tone again. "But we aren't going to need your igloo expertise."

As much as the prince wanted to be mistaken for a normal person, he didn't want this stranger on the mountain thinking she was going to patronize him, and worse, be in charge of things. She seemed to think she was going to protect him, not the other way around. The insult of it was grating.

"We need to think about the baby," he informed her sternly.

She looked astonished. And then she glanced down at the bulge under her jacket, as if she had forgotten her delicate condition. That annoying *amused* smile deepened. Thankfully, it was not accompanied by the chortle, though she looked as if she might be biting it back.

"I have a cabin up here. That's where I was heading. We're ten minutes from there. Let's move."

She had a cabin? A young woman alone on the mountain? A young woman who was about to have a baby? Because of the gathering twilight and the intensity of the snow, the light was growing stranger around them by the moment.

Between that, and the prince standing on the unfamiliar ground of being both unprotected and with someone who had no idea who he was, this whole incident was beginning to have the faint, hazy texture of a dream.

Or a fairy tale.

And then, before his very eyes, the baby bulge her jacket was stretched across moved quite violently!

If that baby decided to arrive, the dream could turn into a nightmare very quickly!

CHAPTER THREE

As VALENTINO GRAPPLED with all of that, Erin set her poles.

"Follow me," she ordered, all business, borderline bossy. "We have to make time. We're losing the light. Try to keep up."

There was that hint of an insult again, both at being given an order and at her instructing him to keep up.

But when he looked down the slope, he was a little shocked by how conditions had diminished suddenly. The snow had thickened to nearly zero visibility, as if the two of them existed alone after being dropped into a milk bottle.

Apparently, she had been right about the storm barely hitting before. Now, it descended on them with its full force. The wind suddenly screamed into the silence, stopped, then screamed again.

He had to raise his voice to be heard above it. "Let's go."

Valentino had been taught by some of the best instructors in the world since he was a small boy. He had skied some of the most exotic places in the world, including the alps of Italy and Switzerland. Skiing to him was like riding. Both activities came as naturally to him as breathing.

He thought Erin should probably be worried about keeping up with him! Particularly in her delicate condition. She would need to protect herself.

But she did not seem to have those concerns. And she quickly proved him wrong about who would be keeping up with whom. She found an almost invisible trail through some trees. Valentino knew he skied well, and maybe extraordinarily so.

But she skied differently than anyone he had ever seen before. Despite the fact she was carrying quite a large pack on her back— and a baby on her front—her movement was both powerful and seemingly effortless. She wasn't conquering the slope of the mountain, she was melding with it, dancing with it, celebrating it.

It was an extraordinary thing to witness, at the same time he was terrified of her falling! He would have shouted at her to slow down, but he never got close enough to make his voice heard above the storm that howled and pulsated around them.

It was also humiliatingly hard to keep up to her. Between the speed she was traveling and the heavily blowing snow creating a blanket between them, it took all his considerable skill to keep her in his sights.

As their passing disturbed them, heavy snow dropped in clumps off the needled branches of the trees. It was like being in a war zone: a sense of life-and-death urgency coupled with the relentless whistling of the wind, snow now dropping from branches like bombs on both sides of the trail.

And then it was over.

Not the storm.

But the sense of urgency and peril. The trail abruptly ended in a small clearing. They had beaten the storm.

Barely visible through the driving snow and ebbing light was a structure. With towering trees at its back, a tiny cabin faced the clearing. It was like something off a Christmas card, the kind of place he thought probably only existed as nostalgia, a figment of imagination, a longing for simplicity and sanctuary in a busy, complex world.

With one last huge effort, he launched himself toward the cabin's promise. They had arrived at safety.

As Valentino stopped at the steps to the cabin, Erin was already stepping out of her bindings and tossing her skis over her shoulder. He felt like a man who had crossed the desert in search of water and could not be certain that what he was seeing was not a mirage. He took it all in.

Constructed of logs, long since weathered to gray, the cabin was anchored on one side by a sturdy chimney made of round, smooth river rocks in varying shades ranging from gold to mauve. In the shadow of a large porch that wrapped around the entire structure, a brightly painted red door welcomed. There were red shutters around the square-paned glass of the windows. The snow, stacked up on the roof, was at least two feet deep.

Valentino was a man who had been raised in grandeur and opulence. The palace of his family was often compared to the Palazzo Brancaccio in Rome, though, as his mother liked to point out to anyone who was interested, it predated that structure by several hundred years. Their house, Palazzo de Oscaro, was arguably the most photographed palace in the Mediterranean.

He followed Erin's suit and kicked off his

skis, and then tumbled, grateful, through the door of the cottage. He had to put his shoulder against it to close it. It was as if the storm was an intruder, demanding to come in with them.

With the storm closed out—howling as if angry at its exclusion—Valentino became aware of a feeling he'd never had before when, at this moment, he felt it for the very first time.

As he leaned his back against the door, he was enveloped in a sense of warmth, a sensation of arriving, finally, after a long, long journey, at the place called home.

But then, sharing the small entryway with him, Erin yanked off her toque and a cascade of hair tumbled out as golden as ripened wheat. She ran her hands through it, tossed it over her shoulder with a shake of her head. He could smell some heady scent.

His sense of having found a safe place, a place called home, evaporated. As someone who had grown up royal, he had had it drummed into him from the first small hop of a hormone: do not *ever* put yourself—and therefore your family—in a compromising position.

In a world that was always under a microscope and always under control, he had never encountered a situation quite like this one.

He was going to be snowed in, alone and entirely unchaperoned, with a woman. A very beautiful woman.

A strange sense of danger, every bit as intense as what he had felt on the mountain and from the storm enveloped him.

A very pregnant woman, Valentino reminded himself. *Thank the gods.*

Valentino on Valentine's Day, Erin thought as she yanked off her toque and ran her hands through her hair, contemplating the option that someone was punking her.

She glanced over her shoulder at the stranger to see if he was amused. An igloo? It had to be a trick of some sort.

But the man looked only relieved to be inside. Besides, who could have put such an elaborate trick in play? It would mean someone had known about Paul breaking off with her. It was possible, given that it had happened two weeks ago, that he was slowly letting people know, even if she was not.

But really? She didn't know anyone in their circle of friends, thank goodness, who was cruel enough to make a joke out of that.

Besides, the whole premise rested on a chance encounter on the mountain. And Valentino seemed to genuinely think she was pregnant. So, no, it had to be the universe having a snicker at her expense.

Well, at least she'd managed to punk back a little bit by letting him believe she was pregnant. And by besting him at skiing. He had skied beautifully, but Erin allowed herself a small snippet of satisfaction that, even so, he couldn't keep up to her.

She patted the bump under her jacket, just to get a reaction from him, but it backfired. The reaction was hers.

Because Valentino lifted his goggles from his eyes.

Any brief satisfaction she had felt by besting him at skiing evaporated like mist before the sun. His eyes were utterly astonishing. A deep, deep brown flecked with gold.

Now that she wasn't, well, taken, and now that they had found sanctuary and safety from the storm, it gave her permission to really look at him as he leaned over and released the buckles on his boots.

She fought the temptation to look at him longer. Instead, she took out the satellite device and tried for a connection. No go. She typed in a quick text to let people know they had arrived safely. Generally, it would send the next time the device found a signal.

She accidentally jostled him as she bent over her own boot buckles.

"Oh, sorry," she said, annoyed that she was blushing as he regained his balance and kicked off the boots.

"I'll set those outside," she said.

He passed the boots to her and his hand brushed hers. She still had her gloves on; he did not. It was impossible that she felt the heat of his touch, wasn't it?

She was so close to him. In the fading light, his golden-toned skin seemed to glow. She could not help but notice his nose: perfect, strong and straight. He had high, commanding cheekbones. He was clean-shaven, which accentuated a faint cleft in his chin, a feature Erin had not realized she found attractive until this very second.

A hint of a dark shadow on his cheeks—added to that exotic skin tone—suggested he might have dark hair beneath the custom-painted ski helmet that complimented the rich navy of his jacket and pants.

For some reason, once her eyes found them, she could not look away from his lips, which were firm and wide. The bottom one was enticingly puffy, the faintest line dividing it in two. What form of madness was this?

Aside from the fact they were going to

be stranded together for at least one night, she was freshly heartbroken! This jolt of pure awareness his lips were causing in her seemed entirely inappropriate.

It felt as if, given the circumstances, she should be ashamed of her awareness of the sensual fullness of his lower lip. She tried to muster that feeling.

Instead, Erin was aware of feeling free, like someone who had been inside a house too long suddenly being let out to breathe fresh air.

It felt liberating, and exhilaratingly so, to just look at a man and appreciate him. It felt good to *not* be taken, spoken for, committed.

Erin was shocked at herself and a new and niggling awareness of how superficial she was capable of being. She turned quickly away from him and put the sets of heavy ski boots outside the door. Snow blew in, right up under the porch. When she stepped back in the door, Valentino had not moved, but was studying the interior of the cabin.

The look on his face was extraordinary. It was as if he was lit from within. Her eyes moved to the puffiness of that lower lip again.

Then he threw back his head and laughed. Was it because he had noticed her fixation on his lips?

"Encantado," he declared softly, his accent unconsciously seductive. And then his eyes came to rest on her. He had spoken in Spanish, so he translated. "I'm enchanted."

She felt as if her breath stopped.

Was he referring to her? To her gazing at his lips? She quickly looked away, over the broadness of his shoulders, and tried to quiet the fluttering of her heart.

All her life she had lived with her father's unending appeal to women, and her mother's bitterness over it. But until this moment, she had not experienced a pull toward someone that felt so compelling. She was shocked to feel something primitive and powerful stir within her.

She had not felt this before—a naked animal awareness of a member of the opposite sex—and it shook her. After all, she knew nothing about this man who was looking so intently at her with a gaze that set fire in her blood.

Wanting.

Wanting what? Erin asked herself primly. She just wasn't the kind of girl who went around lusting after strangers on the ski hill.

Erin did not like weakness. And she particularly did not like *that* weakness. She sighed inwardly. The universe had not only provided her with a Valentino for Valentine's Day, but one that was going to challenge everything she believed about herself.

For instance, that she was not in the least impulsive.

She did not believe people had instincts they could not control.

She certainly did not believe in love at first sight.

He took off his jacket and reached to hang it on a peg behind her. He was very close, in fact, and his presence was so electrical that some of her hair reached out and attached to the sleeve of his white, long-sleeved undershirt.

When she reached out to yank her errant hair back, she realized the undershirt was not wool, but something finer, like alpaca or cashmere. The texture of it made her want to sink her fingers in to it. Or maybe that was the scent that tickled her nostrils, every bit as invigorating as the scent of the coming storm she had detected earlier.

It was faintly spicy, faintly cold, faintly pure man.

Then Valentino removed his ski helmet and reached by her again to put it on a peg. Despite ordering herself not to, Erin could not help but stare at him.

A cascade of damp curls, as black and as shiny as the wings of a raven, had been released from underneath that helmet.

He shook them and then ran a hand through the tangled mop of his hair. He was so gorgeous, it felt as if her heart would stop.

She suddenly was not so sure she did not believe in love at first sight.

That was a thought that had to be resisted wholeheartedly!

"When's the baby due?" he asked, a certain tender protectiveness in his tone that could melt a susceptible person's heart. She was determined she would not be that person.

"I'm not pregnant."

Valentino looked quizzically at her stomach. And then a blush changed the tone of his golden skin. He thought he'd *insulted* her.

Harvey, no doubt recognizing they were home, wanted out. Valentino's eyes widened at the violent wave of motion under her jacket.

She stepped by Valentino into the main room and unzipped her coat to reveal the rounded hump of baby carrier underneath it.

"You skied with a *real* baby?" he breathed, aghast, apparently not familiar enough with baby paraphernalia to realize a head should have been visible if she was, indeed, carrying a real baby.

"Well, my baby."

"But that's not safe!"

"This is the same baby carrier my father used to put me in to come here when I was just a baby," she said. "My family skis as easily as most people walk."

"Still," he said, appalled, "you could have fallen. On your baby."

"Think of it like people in Europe riding bikes with babies in the carriers."

"It's not the same—"

At that moment, Harvey decided he'd had enough. His paws emerged first, over the lip of the carrier. And then he hefted himself up, poking his gray furry head out of the carrier He eyed the stranger in his domain balefully through slitted amber eyes.

Valentino took a startled step back. "That is not a baby!"

"Really?" She looked down at Harvey with pretended astonishment. "Where did he come from?"

Valentino eyed her with such annoyance, a shiver went up and down her spine. He had that look of a man far too certain of himself, a man that people did not cross.

"You're not pregnant," he said, something edgy in his voice.

"Is there any reason you would sound disappointed by that news?"

"You let me believe it. You let me think I might be delivering a baby in an igloo."

"I'm in no way responsible for other people's absurd conclusions!"

"You're skiing with a cat and you call me absurd?" he shot back.

"I don't think I would have been out here skiing by myself if I was that close to having a baby. What do you take me for? An idiot?"

"I feel as if I've been the one played for the idiot," he said stiffly. "You could have told me right away. Plus, you could have seriously injured your animal."

"Not just an idiot! An irresponsible idiot! Believe me, if I had fallen on Harvey, I would have come out of it in worse shape than him."

Valentino looked at her with narrowed eyes. She could feel a spark in the air between them. She didn't like sparks between people! She liked calm.

But look where that liking had gotten her. Paul had told her, in his little breakup speech, that their relationship was boring. It reminded him of his mother and father's relationship. It was obvious—look at her relationship with Harvey—that she wanted children. Soon.

He wasn't ready. Kids and family felt like jail to him.

Erin's focus moved again to the intrigue of that puffy split in Valentino's bottom lip. She contemplated the feeling that rippled through her. Whatever it was, it was not boring.

She was annoyed with him. He was aggravated with her. And still, underneath that ran a current of…something. Something she could not encourage, or investigate, given their circumstances.

Not that she would want to under any circumstances. That kind of spark was dangerous! It could burn a whole forest down before you even blinked.

They were about to be snowed in here, together, for who knew how long. There was no room in that equation for *wanting*.

CHAPTER FOUR

THERE WAS NO room for wanting, Erin told herself sternly, no matter how delectable Valentino's lips were. Part of her, to her own disgust, sighed. *What would one little taste hurt?*

There would be no such thing as a *little* taste of those lips. It would be like trying to have only one little bite of fantastic chocolate.

And there was no room for attractions or sparky arguments, either, even if it did make her feel faintly invigorated.

"Let's call a truce," she suggested. *And not look at each other's lips.* "I'm sorry I let you believe I might be pregnant."

"For your own amusement," he said.

"You obviously did not get the script," she told him with elaborate and sarcastic patience. "This is the part where you say, 'I'm sorry I insinuated you were an irresponsible idiot.'"

Valentino was silent. He looked stern. Almost forbidding. A man who rarely had to give an inch to anyone and who didn't plan to now.

"I have food," she told him. "And wine. And I'm not above bribing you for a truce."

"I'm bigger than you. I could just take them." But finally the stern line around his mouth softened.

"But you wouldn't," she said.

He cocked his head at her.

"I can tell by looking at you. And since we're stuck here together for a while, it would probably be better if we made an attempt to be civil. So, truce?"

He considered. He nodded. "Truce."

Having won that reluctant concession from Valentino, Erin released the cat from the carrier and set him on the floor. Harvey would have normally headed straight to his dish and complained loudly at finding it empty. Instead, he marched over, tail high, and wound himself around Valentino's legs.

Despite her call for a truce, she couldn't believe her cat.

Traitor.

She could usually count on Harvey to be an equal opportunities hater. He had held Paul in utter contempt for the entire length of their relationship.

Valentino squatted and scratched under the

scruffy cat's chin. "You look like an old warrior," he said.

She was suddenly not so sure how wise calling a truce had been. Valentino's deep voice, roughened with affection, sent a tingle up and down her spine. If she was not mistaken, her cranky cat was reacting about the same way. He rounded his back as Valentino's hands moved from his chin to his tail.

Erin stared at his hands. They were not the hands of a working man, but rather beautifully shaped and manicured while still being entirely masculine. He must be an executive. Actually, given that take-charge, brook-no-nonsense demeanor, she was willing to bet he owned and ran a very successful company.

He was doing something with those hands—caressing—that made that *wanting* leap to the fore more powerfully than when she had first fought it back.

The cat preened under his touch.

"How old is he?" Valentino asked, not the least bit aware, thank goodness, that she had become entranced with his hands.

"I've had him since I was eleven," she said. "And he wasn't a kitten, then, so he's at least fifteen, maybe older."

"And you travel with him?"

Was she eager to let him know she was not

some eccentric single woman who could not be separated from her cat? It would seem so. But, wait a second, wasn't she the one who had decided to embrace the single life?

Looking at Valentino's hands on that cat, she was embarrassingly aware she didn't want to be perceived as a career single person and a crazy cat lady!

"He's going slowly blind," Erin explained. "And deaf. He's nervous when I'm not around, so I've increasingly found ways to keep him close to me. He sleeps most of the time now, so it's no problem to have him under my desk at work. I'm in accounting at the resort."

"Accounting?"

Was she relieved at the surprise in his voice? When had she started being a person who didn't want to look like she was in accounting?

About half an hour ago!

"Yes, accounting. Harvey is kind of the office mascot, even though he has a nasty streak."

"A nasty streak?" Valentino said, giving Harvey's chin another scratch before straightening. "I don't believe it."

Harvey cast her a look that clearly said he'd been *seen*.

"That's an unusual amount of dedication to a pet on your part," he said.

Paul had thought it was distinctly weird, not admirable.

"I owe him one," Erin said. She went over to the kitchen counter and removed some long matches from a jar.

"That's interesting. How can you owe a cat something? I would think it might be the other way around. You provide for him. Food. Shelter. Tummy rubs."

"No, it's definitely me that owes him." She began to move around the room, opening the valves on the wall lamps and lighting them, one by one, until the room took on a soft glow. It was full dark outside now and the lights made the cabin seem like a cozy nest in the middle of the storm that raged right outside the windows.

"What can I do?"

"Could you feed Harvey? His food is in the top drawer over there and his dish is beside the fridge."

Valentino crossed the room, telepathic cat on his heels, and Erin could not help but notice the grace and athleticism she had seen on the mountain was still very evident in the way he moved. He carried himself with supreme confidence. He found the one-serve cat food and broke one open.

Harvey, at the sound of the package opening, yowled as if he hadn't been fed for a week. Valentino, somehow at home, rummaged around in another drawer until he found a spoon, leaned over the dish and scraped the food into it.

Harvey, impatient, kept pushing his hand out of the way, until Valentino laughed.

Erin retrieved her backpack and began taking its contents out. She left the bakery box with the heart-shaped cake in the pack. She had bought a candle for it that was shaped like the number one. She had planned a defiant celebration of finding herself single by having a Valentine's Day feast for one. Now, she didn't know what was going to happen. If the storm abated overnight, in the morning she would be taking Valentino down the slopes. Would she come back up? Somehow, celebrating being single on Valentine's Day had lost its appeal.

And if he was still there, she was not sure a Valentine's Day feast would be appropriate.

It occurred to Erin that it had been a long time since she had shifted a plan spontaneously. A long time since things had gone out of control in her world.

She told herself she liked it that way, the plans and predictability. That's why she worked in accounting. The world of numbers was safe and regulated. You applied formulas and got expected outcomes.

And yet, if she were honest, wasn't she rather enjoying this scenario?

Of not knowing what would happen next? Of things being slightly out of her control? Wasn't life suddenly and unexpectedly infused with a sense of adventure? Didn't it feel oddly and wonderfully exhilarating to be ensconced inside the cabin—stranded—with a gorgeous stranger?

Maybe that had been missing from her life.

Maybe Paul was correct when he had declared it all a little too dull and predictable, too boring. Maybe they had been—she had been—too young for that, to be acting like his parents.

"Steak it is," she muttered. Some of the items needed to go in the fridge and again she found herself in close quarters with Valentino.

The problem was, was her sanctuary ever going to feel the same after this? Or would his substantial presence—his laughter—leave a mark here, like a shadow?

He watched, grinning, as the cat gulped

down the food. "There's no possible way you owe him," he decided.

"I do."

"Like he saved you from a burning building or something like that?"

"Something very like that," she said. "I've heard that you do not choose a cat, a cat chooses you."

Because of Paul's almost instant animosity to the cat, Erin had never told him that part, never trusted him with her vulnerability around the cat. Harvey wasn't just her pet. He was her family.

She moved quickly out of the kitchen, adjusted the thermostat in the living room and heard the comforting chuff of the propane-powered furnace kicking over. She finally shrugged off her coat and removed the carrier.

"Electric heat," he said, his surprise evident in his voice. But when she glanced at him, he didn't seem that interested in the furnace.

His eyes rested for a moment on her and she was glad for her choice of this sweater— white angora—this morning. It flattered her, a sweater that said—if sweaters could say such things—*Is this the sweater of a woman who has just been thrown over by her boyfriend?*

"Propane, but it does the trick. It's quite a modern igloo," she told him, annoyed at herself for being glad about the sweater. "We even have an indoor bathroom."

"Okay," he said, holding up his hands, cowboy surrender. "I think we've moved on from the igloo stuff. It's in the terms of the truce."

"I'll have to see a written copy."

His laugh, again, was so delightful. Warm. It filled the space with its richness and vibrancy.

"Anyway, I get it," he continued. "All the modern conveniences. No igloo stereotype. It actually seems more like something out of a fairy tale than an igloo."

Valentino was looking around with very real interest, and Erin followed his gaze, trying to see the familiar space through the eyes of a stranger.

"You mustn't be much of an expert on fairy tales," she told him, trying for a light tone. "Don't they usually take place in castles?"

With a prince, she reminded herself. It was embarrassingly easy to envision him, with his very evident confidence and composure, and with that exotic lovely accent, as the kind of prince who rode through the pages of fairy tales rescuing damsels in distress.

That, given her recent breakup, she might qualify as.

"Ah, castles," Valentino said with a shake of his head, pretending to be a man weary of such things. It was her turn to laugh.

He grinned back at her.

"This seems much preferable. The gingerbread cottage that Hansel and Gretel found in the woods," he elaborated.

She was sure her place on the mountain was just like thousands of other Canadian cottages, and yet she loved this space so much. A big stone fireplace dominated the room, the rough-hewn timber mantel littered with dusty ski trophies. Cozy furniture, covered in carelessly tossed plaid throws, circled around it, and stuffed bookshelves flagged both sides. An L-shaped kitchen with knotty-pine lower cabinets and open-shelving uppers took up one corner of the not very big space.

The main living area of the cabin was all one room, but this expanse inside the door had a large square of tile that could handle snow melting off clothes better than wood. On the wall behind the door was an abundance of pegs to hang wet clothing.

Still, the kitchen space suddenly seemed very tight. Erin was aware, again, of his size. Not just that he was taller than she, but that the sizzling masculine energy of him made her feel almost small and decidedly feminine. Small was something she had rarely felt! She had been five foot nine inches by the time she was fourteen.

His gaze fell on her and he smiled. "Minus the wicked child-eating witch, of course."

"Don't underestimate Harvey."

Just like that, they were laughing together, the soft light from the lanterns illuminating his skin tone, his mouth, his hair.

The man was absolutely, stunningly, gorgeous.

Gorgeous, and yet Erin was aware of that feeling again, that she had seen him before. She must have caught a glimpse of him in the village, though that didn't feel quite right. He did not seem like the kind of man a person—even one who'd had her dreams of a ring for Valentine's Day dashed—would forget seeing.

"What?" he asked her softly, and she realized, embarrassed, she was not just staring but being very obvious about it. She looked away quickly.

"I'm not sure. You look familiar," Erin admitted, glancing back at him.

"Do I?" he asked. Did the faintest of shutters lower over those amazing eyes? Was he being deliberately unforthcoming, as if he was accustomed to being recognized?

She realized he might be a model: that's how gorgeous he was. Maybe she had seen him in a glossy magazine, in one of those supersexy ads for men's cologne or out-of-reach holidays on tropical beaches.

Except his sexiness was threaded through with a distinct dignity she was fairly certain was not for sale.

A film star, then? No, that wasn't quite right, either. Though he definitely had a star quality, a presence, he simply did not seem, in their short acquaintance, like a man who could pretend to be someone else for a living.

"You're probably mistaking me for Sebastian Avio," he said, naming a famous Mediterranean opera singer. His tone teasing, he said, "Lots of people do."

Only if Sebastian were thirty years younger than Valentino was, Erin thought.

"You should take off your pants," she said, trying to shift her awareness of him and seeing they were shedding a puddle on the floor.

"I bet you only say that to guys who remind you of Sebastian Avio," he said, his tone still teasing.

She could feel heat moving up her cheeks. Surely, she could have thought of another way to word that? She didn't have to act as if she was a gauche schoolgirl in the presence of her secret crush.

"I'll expect you to serenade me later," she said, hoping to hide her discomfort with a bit of banter.

She didn't think she'd succeeded. He seemed faintly amused by her lack of composure and though he dropped the suspenders off his shoulders—making her even more aware of the broadness of them—he made no move to take off his ski pants. She realized, the heat growing in her cheeks, that if he only had an undershirt on under the jacket, that might be all he had on under the pants, too.

She turned away from him, vacating that tight-shared square of space as if she were in danger of catching fire. And it felt like she was!

"Go in to that second bedroom over there." She gestured at one of the doors off the main room. "There should be some clothes that will fit you in the closet."

"Thank you," he said.

"I'll just get the fire going," she said. "It will help warm it up more quickly in here and save on propane."

Not that she felt chilly. Embarrassingly warm, actually.

She busied herself with that, not looking at him as he moved by her, concentrating on preparing the paper and the kindling as if her life depended on it.

Something tingled at the back of her neck and Erin was aware that Valentino had not gone through to the back bedroom.

"'Enrique O'Rourke,'" he read off the trophies. "Wow."

"You know him?" she asked carefully.

"Of him. Who doesn't? A legend."

"My father," she admitted. "My grandfather started this resort."

"That explains it."

"Explains what?"

"Being allowed to keep a cat under your desk, for one. Your access to this Hansel and Gretel cabin in the middle of nowhere, for another. But more than that, how you ski. To be honest, when you first told me to try and keep up, I almost laughed out loud."

She turned to look at him and allowed herself a small smile. "I know. I could tell."

"Then that must have made it extra delightful for you to leave me eating your snow all the way here."

"It did," she said. And then they both laughed. The shared laughter, again, should have eased some tension she was feeling but it did not. It made her more aware of him, how easy and natural it felt to laugh with him. "You made me work at it, though. Leaving you eating my snow."

"I can swallow my pride for Enrique O'Rourke's daughter. I've never seen anybody ski like you. Except maybe him, now that I think about it."

"Thanks," she said. "He taught me, so our styles should be similar."

"It's as if you're folding yourself into the mountain somehow. Not on top of it, but part of it."

Was it his accent that made the words feel like pure poetry? Whatever it was, it was lovely to be admired.

She felt hungry for it. Almost pathetically so. Her father had been stingy with compliments. And so had Paul.

She frowned. Was there a connection there?

"My father really never forgave me when I didn't want a career in skiing," she said then wondered what on earth had made her say that. It seemed way too personal.

But she glanced over her shoulder at Valentino again. He seemed to be contemplating her words gravely.

"I think maybe it is the nature of growing

up to want different things than our parents," he said. "Be grateful you had a choice."

And then he, too, looked regretful, as if he had said too much or revealed too much.

Valentino left the room quickly. But no matter how she tried to concentrate on the fire in front of her, it felt as if another fire was starting.

Deep inside her.

Ridiculous, she told herself. She would not be so weak and facile as to drown her sorrows over her recently shattered dreams in the deep and inviting sea of a stranger's charm.

She would not see it as a gift from the universe that she was stranded on the eve of Valentine's Day with someone named Valentino.

No. More like a test.

A challenge.

A trial of her strength of character.

One that she was resolved to pass.

CHAPTER FIVE

VALENTINO MADE HIS way down the hall to the bedroom. He was glad to be leaving the room that Erin was in. He was so *aware* of her. Her scent, the melody of her voice, the way that spun-with-gold hair tumbled over her shoulders, the sweet cling of that sweater.

But perhaps that awareness served as a distraction, because he was dealing with extremely weighty issues. He had escaped to Canada, to the Touch-the-Clouds resort, to make a decision.

In two weeks, his engagement to Angelica, princess of the neighboring island kingdom of Sorrento, was to be declared. The engagement event would be huge: a dinner where the formal announcement would be made, followed by a ball.

The palace had been in a frenzy of preparation for a month. And the people of Lorenzo knew it was coming. Never had there been a people so eager to celebrate life, and this would be their day, as well as his and Angelica's. Families would be picnicking on the palace grounds in anticipation of the balcony door opening, the king and queen stepping out onto it, he and Angelica following... They would cry for that first kiss, and their applause and cheers when it happened would be like a tidal wave of sound.

Angelica and Valentino had known each other since they were children. Their union was expected—it had been negotiated at her birth. He was now twenty-seven; she was twenty-two. The pressure had been building for two years. It was *time*.

He liked Angelica, and she liked him, in that comfortable way of old friends who had common ground and much of it. With her massive dark curls and her ready smile, she was beautiful, she was smart, and she was funny.

As far as arranged marriages went, Valentino was aware he had hit the jackpot.

And yet...he was chafing against this choice being made for him. Still, he had been raised with a sense of duty and service. The needs of his island kingdom came before his own, and the alliance with Sorrento was imperative.

So why was he here? Why had he run away for a break in Canada? What good could it do? His fate was cast.

Valentino knew he would have accepted that. It was Angelica who had made him need to get away from it all. To clear his head. To gain perspective. To make a decision.

Their encounters, since they had hit puberty, had been closely chaperoned, and that day a week ago had been no different. Angelica had suggested a ride so that they could speak privately, the chaperone trailing behind them on a forest path.

Angelica loved to ride. She rode well and aggressively, but that day she had been subdued. He could tell Angelica's spark was being snuffed. She was *so* unhappy.

He had probed the unhappiness and, casting a guarded glance back, she had admitted she didn't feel ready to get married. She didn't feel ready to surrender to the expectations, which would be to produce a royal heir as soon as humanly possible.

"Don't take it personally," she had pleaded with him. "I love you, Valentino, but like a brother. I want to *feel* things. I want to feel so in love that it's as if I can't breathe when I'm not with that other person. I want to feel passion so hot, I become the flame, consumed by the heat of another person's touch."

It was his turn to cast a wary glance back at the chaperone. Because it was evident to him that Angelica already had met someone who made her feel exactly those things.

If she was already acting on them—and because of the flush in her cheeks and the smoldering in her dark eyes, of that he was fairly certain—she was going to do something rash.

If he called off the engagement before it was announced, could he protect her, a least a little bit, from the outrage and disappointment such a breakup would bring on the instigator? Would such a move actually free her or would her parents make new arrangements for her immediately?

Where did the good of his own kingdom fit into all of this? He was an only child. He knew—and was reminded constantly—the royal legacy fell on him.

He sighed, rolled his shoulders, trying to relieve the weight on them. He opened the closet door and looked at the clothing offerings, which seemed to lean toward plaid shirts and blue jeans.

A few minutes later, feeling as if he was in the most ridiculous costume, he went back out to the main room.

Erin, who had pinned her hair up into a loose bun, was in the kitchen. She glanced at him and grinned. He had the renegade thought that he wanted to free her hair, to pull those pins from it, one by one.

Valentino had always prided himself on his intense discipline, and so the wayward thought took him aback.

"You look very Canadian! You could pass yourself off as a lumberjack."

"My greatest ambition," he said, his tone deliberately dry with no hint of *I want to pull the pins from your hair* in it. "I thought we were going to avoid Canadian stereotypes?"

She seemed to think about it. "Hmm. Is it in the agreement? Because, at the moment, you actually look like someone who could make an igloo."

He frowned at her. "I thought we had decided to leave that behind us?"

"I still haven't seen a written version," she teased him.

He contemplated that. Being teased. He decided he liked it, even as it made keeping a cool distance between them more difficult.

She glanced at him. "Okay, Val, come and make yourself useful."

Val? Make yourself useful? Again, Valentino was not sure he had ever been addressed quite like that in his life.

"How can I assist?" he asked.

"You can open the wine, and then I've got ingredients for a Mediterranean salad. You look like you'd be an expert on both those things."

Valentino was not sure what would make him look like an expert on such things. The truth was, he had never opened a bottle of wine himself and he had certainly never made a salad. Mediterranean or otherwise. He was aware of a strange tension at the back of his neck, as if this were a test he needed to pass.

He went over to where the bottle of wine was on the kitchen table, trying to appear casual, like this was a workaday event for him. He regarded the bottle. It felt like the enemy.

He picked it up, trying to buy some time, studying the label. "A white," he said. "Sauvignon."

"It's a Canadian wine. From a British Columbian vineyard. I try to buy local. And I avoid screw caps."

All the more shame, he thought as he tentatively peeled away a silver-foil seal that revealed a cork firmly embedded in the neck of the bottle.

"The corkscrew is in the drawer over there." Erin gestured with her head.

The drawer was on the other side. He moved by her. Her scent tickled his nostrils. She was seasoning a steak. Thank goodness, it looked as if one of them knew what they were doing.

He opened the drawer she had pointed to. It was full of items he didn't recognize, most of which looked like they had been designed to compel confessions in the torture chamber. The corkscrew, thankfully, was easily recognizable as the instrument used by the palace sommelier to open wine at the table.

Valentino grabbed it and went back to the bottle. He'd seen wine opened a zillion times, even if he had never done it himself. Confident now, he jammed the sharp tip into the cork. Then, putting a bit of weight on it, he twisted. Instead of coming out, the cork seemed to recede deeper beneath the lip and down the neck of the bottle. He must not have made sure the corkscrew was seated firmly enough. He pressed harder. The cork moved in the wrong direction.

The last time he'd opened a bottle of wine, it had been to smash it across the hull of a ship he had been invited to christen.

He had, on several official occasions, seen

champagne uncorked with a sword. Valentino slid Erin a look. She wasn't paying the least bit of attention to him.

He bet uncorking a champagne bottle with a sword would impress her.

Did he *want* to impress her?

What man didn't want to impress a beautiful woman? And maybe, in that realization, he had already made up his mind about Angelica and what he needed to do. Because his entire life, he had been *taken,* and so had not felt awareness of women the way he now felt it about Erin.

Was it because of their circumstances? Escaping the storm, followed by the intense solitude of the situation he found himself in with a woman who was a stranger to him?

Or was it because, somewhere along the line—maybe from the moment he had stepped on the royal plane headed for Canada—he had already known what he'd needed to do.

"How's that coming?"

He put more weight into the corkscrew. The cork groaned down the neck of the bottle, letting loose suddenly and splashing into the wine, where it floated, baleful evidence of his failure.

"Um…done," he said, turning to her, blocking her view of the bottle with his body.

"Great. Can you start the salad? I'm just going to run out and turn on the grill. Unless you'd rather do that and I'll do the salad?"

He looked at the heap of ingredients on the kitchen counter at her elbow: colorful peppers, cucumbers, tiny tomatoes, olives, a block of white Feta cheese.

Everything was whole. He wasn't sure where to even begin tackling the vegetables. On the other hand, a grill? It sounded like a good way to blow them both up.

"I'm fine with the salad," he lied.

"Knives are in the block there."

She picked up the steak and opened the side door to a small porch. Wind tossed snow in before she quickly stepped out then nudged the door shut again with her hip.

He went over to the block and took out a knife. It was a huge, heavy thing that looked as if it might be good for a beheading. A pepper? Not so much. One by one, Valentino took out the knives and studied them. Finally, in the interest of self-preservation, he chose the least lethal-looking one.

Carefully, he cut the pepper in two and was astonished to find *stuff* inside it. He'd been unaware peppers contained *contents*.

Were the contents—tiny seeds and felt-like bits—part of the salad? He didn't recall ever seeing anything that looked like that in a salad before. He tested a seed and pared off some of the felty substance. He sampled that, too. It tasted just like a pepper to him. Was it possible he hadn't seen it in a salad before because of some form of *snobbery*? Surely common people ate everything that tasted good? Having revealed his own privilege to himself, he carefully chopped up the remainder of the pepper, including all its parts, and tossed it in the bowl Erin had provided.

The wind shook the cabin. He wished she would come in out of it. He should have volunteered to do the grilling. He didn't like it that she was out there and he was in here.

He abandoned the salad and went to the door. The wind pulled it out of his hands.

"Can I help you?" he asked her. "We could switch, if you're cold."

"No, almost done," she said, apparently unbothered by the wind and snow whistling around her. Delectable smells drifted to him. "How's the salad?"

"Great," he said, "I could probably have my own cooking show."

Wouldn't that give his mother conniptions? Still, Erin laughed, and he liked that.

He returned to the kitchen and focused on the block of Feta cheese. He was feeling quite pleased with how easy it all was when his knife hand slipped. He stared down at the cutting board in a kind of paralyzed horror.

Unless he was mistaken, that was a tiny tip of his finger sitting there among the crumbled cheese and red-pepper juices. He looked at his finger.

Blood was gushing from it.

The door opened. "Steak is done," she sang.

He turned to her, slowly, holding up his hand.

"I seem to have had a small mishap. It doesn't bode well for my cooking show," he said.

She dropped the platter holding the steak. It landed on the floor with a clatter, and she rushed to him. She took his hand in her own.

He considered how all he should have felt was pain. But the pain had not set in yet and what he felt was her touch. Cool. Comforting.

"Let's just get that up," she said, guiding his hand to a more elevated position. Then she led him over to the couch. "Sit down. I'll get the first-aid kit. I think it's in the medicine cabinet. Don't worry. It's nothing."

He didn't feel worried at all, but he heard something shrill in her voice.

Erin tossed a dish towel at him. "It's clean," she said, "wrap it around your finger."

She looked pale and shaky as she disappeared down the hallway. Meanwhile, the cat had launched himself on the steak that had fallen to the floor and greedily had his face buried in it.

He got up and rescued the steak from the cat, who was clearly furious to have his prize taken from him. Valentino set the steak on the counter.

"Here it is," she said, coming back, waving a white, tin first-aid kit triumphantly. "What are you doing? You need to be sitting down." The shrillness in her voice had increased.

"It's just a scratch," he told her mildly.

"It's not!" she said. "Sit!"

He sat. She knelt at his feet and placed the kit on a hassock. She rummaged through it. He studied the top of her head, the sun-threaded gold of her hair. One of those pins that was holding that bun together was loose. Just the tiniest nudge with his finger…

"There," she said. She had items laid out on the hassock like a field doctor preparing to do surgery. She closed her eyes, inhaled a deep breath, and opened them again.

She took his hand in hers. She was trembling as she peeked inside the dish towel. He was the one who was hurt!

The towel had become quite saturated with

blood in a very short time and, if it were possible, Erin paled even more.

"Are you afraid of blood?" he asked.

"I'm afraid you're going to bleed to death," she said, but the denial was weak.

"You're afraid of blood."

"I don't think *afraid* is the right word," she said, not denying it this time. Well, how could she? Her face was as white as that snow outside and she was trembling. "But—"

She took another deep, fortifying breath and finished unwrapping the dish towel from his hand. Blood spurted out the end of his finger. She hastily wrapped it again.

"I can do it myself," he said.

"No! I'll do it." She took off the towel again. This time she had a wipe ready and quickly cleaned the wound. It looked as if he had managed to remove the entire pad from the tip of his finger.

"Hey," he said, "that'll be handy if I commit a crime. No fingerprints."

She did not seem amused at his attempt to distract. Her face determined, her tongue caught between her teeth, she began to wind gauze tightly around his entire finger, crisscrossing the tip. His finger was beginning to look like a marshmallow, but she was being so brave—for him—that he said nothing.

Finally, she reached for her carefully laid-out medical tape, leaned close and began to wind it around his finger. He couldn't help it... He reached for that errant pin, felt the silk of her hair under his fingertips.

Pulling that pin was like pulling one card from a shaky house of them. Her hair tumbled down.

Much better, he thought.

She glanced up at him, wide-eyed, her eyes as green as a piece of perfect jade catching the light.

"It was falling out," he lied.

He immediately felt contrite. She looked even worse than before, shaky as an olive tree leaf in a faint breeze. Of course she would look like that! A strange man removing pins from her hair. It was a terrible faux pas.

"Here," he said, getting up, crouching beside her, putting his shoulder under her. "Your turn to sit. Let me look after dinner."

"You're the injured one," she protested, though her protest lacked vehemence.

He held out his gigantic white-wrapped finger to her. "All fixed. I'll take it from here. You relax. Thank you for doing that. Especially since you are afraid of blood."

"Since I was a child," she admitted.

Thank goodness! Her current state of wooziness seemed to have nothing to do with his fingers, acting separately from his brain, reaching for her hair.

Given the intensity of the circumstances, he had to make sure he didn't do anything so inappropriate again.

Valentino spun away from Erin, eager to put a bit of distance between them while he regained his sanity.

CHAPTER SIX

ERIN WATCHED AS Valentino moved away to the humble kitchen. She should protest his offering to get dinner, especially now that he was handicapped with a giant, white-wrapped finger. Maybe she had gotten a little carried away with the first aid—but she hadn't wanted any blood to leak through that bandage. She felt woozy enough already.

Embarrassingly, she had been dizzy even before he had touched her hair. Good grief, she had gone from faintly light-headed to full swoon in the blink of an eye.

Harvey stalked him into the kitchen and waited, hopefully, under the counter for a drop. There was something endearing about watching Valentino in the kitchen. For a man with such grace and athleticism on the ski hill, he now looked like a duck out of water, completely unsure of himself.

After contemplating his options for a mo-

ment, he started with the steak, which he in-
spected. He rinsed it under the tap and then
blotted it. She remembered it had fallen on
the floor.

"You were planning this meal for yourself
only," he noted, cutting the steak, which was
not large, in two. "Thank you for sharing your
supper with me."

"Of course!" she said. She was glad the
heart-shaped cake with its embarrassing *"1"*
candle was still hidden in her pack. "The
dressing for the salad is in the fridge."

As she watched, he finished up the salad
and then plated the food and poured them
each a glass of wine. He found a metal tray
and put everything on it. Balancing it carefully, he brought it over to her. He shoved
aside her first-aid supplies on the hassock,
set the tray down and settled on the couch.

The couch wasn't large—more like a love
seat—and his thigh touched hers. An electrical current of awareness jolted through her.

"M'lady," he said. He leaned over and took
a wineglass off the tray with the hand that
was not bandaged. He awkwardly handed it
to her. He took the other one.

"A toast," he said.

She lifted her glass.

"To surprises."

"To surprises," she agreed.

They clinked glasses and she took a sip, as did he.

"This is really a nice wine," he said. "It's dry but fruity. I almost get an overtone of lime in it."

He seemed to know quite a bit more about wine than she did. To her distress, Erin felt something chunky in her mouth. She tried to figure out what it was and what to do. She had an awful decision to make. Spit it out or swallow it?

"Ah, there was a little problem with the cork," he said, noticing her expression just as she made a decision to swallow.

"It happens," she said, setting down the glass. He handed her a plate and some utensils. She regarded his offer solemnly, took her fork and poked through the pepper part of the salad. It seemed, like the wine, to have foreign components in it.

He was watching her, eager for her to sample it.

"Oh, sorry, I was just wondering—"

"Yes?"

"What exactly is this?"

He regarded the item she was holding on her fork. "Pepper insides." He blinked at her with elaborate innocence. "Don't you use them?"

"Not generally."

"We do. In my country."

She felt her lips twitch at so obvious a lie. "Don't take up poker," she suggested.

"I happen to be an excellent poker player!"

"Have you ever made a salad before?"

"I have not," he admitted. His lips twitched, too.

"Or cut vegetables?"

"No."

"It's a good thing I didn't ask you to chop wood," she decided. "You probably would have lost a hand."

"Except for the fact that's true, I'd be insulted," he said.

"What exactly were you planning on doing if I had a baby?"

"Boil water!"

And then they were both laughing.

The steak, despite his running it under the tap, had grit in it, The wine had the odd piece of cork, and the seed-ridden salad was possibly the chunkiest she had ever eaten.

But with the storm deepening and howling outside, and the warmth and the wine inside, it felt so good. As good as anything in Erin's life had felt for a long, long time.

Valentino took away their plates and fetched the rest of the wine. He refilled their glasses.

"Tell me about where you're from," she invited. A voice inside her added, *And what you do, and who you love. Valentino, tell me every little intriguing thing about you.*

"I come from a small island in the Mediterranean, Lorenzo del Toro. Have you heard of it?"

Had she? She thought so, but the wine and the warmth of the fire, her stomach full, his gaze touching her face, made her not very sure of anything about the world. "I'm not sure."

"Ah, well, let me take you there." And just like that, his voice swept her from the little cottage and the storm that raged outside the door.

They were in a sun-drenched land of olive groves and vineyards, ancient buildings and quaint stone cottages and cobbled streets. The flowers were so colorful and so abundant that the air was perfumed by them. Donkeys pulling carts and shepherds herding sheep blocked narrow country roads.

"And what do you do there?"

"I'm in the family business," he said. Did she hear a note of caution in his voice?

"And what is your family business?"

Again, did she sense hesitation?

Valentino took a sip of wine. He refilled her glass. He looked at the fire. "We manage a number of enterprises," he finally said. "The business is hundreds of years old."

"Do you like it?"

He thought about that for a minute. "I'm not sure I've ever thought of it in terms of liking or not liking. It is what I was born into."

"That's what you meant when you said to be grateful I had a choice about whether or not to follow in my father's footsteps? That you did not? That you were expected to go into the family business?"

"Yes," he said. "That's what I meant. But enough about me now. Tell me about you. About growing up with a father like yours."

Maybe it was because of the wine. Or maybe it was because their experience was a little like being trapped with a stranger on an elevator given the relentless storm outside, but there was a kind of instant intimacy developing between them. However, there was a time limit on this.

He lived around the world in a place she was never likely to go. After the storm abated, she was probably never going to see him again.

Why did that feel, already, like a sadness?

Still, Erin found herself confiding in him

about growing up in the crazy world of professional skiing with a very famous father.

"I had skis on practically as soon as I could walk. And I loved to ski—and still do. It's my place where I feel one hundred percent engaged. Present. Alive.

"But, to my father's great disappointment, I wasn't interested in putting my natural ability, which I had inherited from him and my grandfather before him, to work for me. I'd raced since I was tiny. When you're small and everyone gets a trophy, it was fine, and fun.

"But I grew to hate it," she said softly. "There was too much pressure on me because I was the great Enrique's daughter.

"Remember when Sebastian Avio's daughter wanted a career in music? And everyone kept comparing her to him? It was like that. I mean… I was just a kid and I was being interviewed on the evening news after a race.

"Plus, even at the junior levels—we're talking under ten—racing brought out this horrible competitive side in my dad. He became my mentor and my coach. I could do nothing right. If I won a race, he started dissecting how I could have done better immediately. If I lost, he'd be furious, pouting and sulking.

"It took what I loved the most and changed it into something I could barely recognize. So, at age eleven, I stood firm and told him I was leaving my career as a ski racer behind me. I quit. Nothing was ever the same between us after that, as if he couldn't handle it that my life didn't belong to him.

"In retrospect, with everything going on in the family, I think ski racing had become just one more pressure. One I was ill-prepared to handle."

"What was going on in your family?"

Erin thought she had really said quite enough. And yet there was something about the way he was looking at her and listening to her that felt like an elixir: if she drank of this cup, she would feel better.

That was astonishing because she hadn't been aware she *wasn't* feeling okay. Harvey jumped on her lap and she scratched his ears. Valentino reached over and scratched his ears, too.

It was such a nice moment. It had a lovely intimacy to it. Their total isolation from the whole world made her feel as if she could tell him anything.

Not just as if she could tell him anything, but as if she had carried a burden too long by herself and this stranger had come along and unexpectedly offered to share it.

During the tumultuous years of her childhood, and just before they'd called it quits for good, her parents' relationship had been more volatile than ever.

"My mother," she said softly, "had just discovered my father had yet another love interest. The days were filled with the sounds of slammed doors and shouted arguments. So many accusations and so much pain. Love that had burned too hot had finally consumed everything in its flame, destroying everything around it."

Erin cast a look at Valentino. That's where mooning over someone's lips got you. That was where passion led.

"That's why I said I owed the cat," she confessed. "Harvey chose me. He showed up on our doorstep and became my shadow, just when I needed him most. Even back then, when he was young and handsome, silky-furred and svelte, Harvey hated absolutely everyone. Except me.

"This silly old guy reserved his absolute devotion for me, at the time in my life when I could do nothing right in my father's eyes and our family unit was exploding around me. Maybe some people—maybe most people—would see my loyalty to the cat as odd, but he gave me hope when the world seemed utterly hopeless.

"The cat was my constant as I moved between my parents' ever-shifting households, partners, locations.

"I fell asleep at night, in whichever house I was in, often with my pillow soaked in tears. But the cat curled in close to me, his purr reassuring and solid."

Solid. Stable.

She cast a glance at Valentino. His hand had gone still on the cat's fur. He was frowning at the fire.

She had said *way* too much.

But when he looked away from the fire and at her, his dark eyes were even darker, shadowed with sadness, as if he had, indeed, taken some of her burden as his own. Erin felt something she had not felt for so long.

A trust in this man beside her unfurled within her.

"And tell me," he said softly, "what all this has to do with you and your cat bringing a feast up here to have Valentine's Day alone."

She wasn't sure if she hated it or loved it. That he saw, immediately, how her tumultuous childhood and being alone right now were linked.

"Naturally, after all that excitement and chaos growing up, I longed for what other people seemed to have. Family as a place of refuge. Calm.

"I thought I was going to build that with my boyfriend, Paul, because his family was the polar opposite of mine. A mother and father who never seemed to say a cross word after thirty years together. Who had roast chicken on Sunday nights. Who belonged to the bowling league.

"What I didn't realize was that while I'd been enchanted with all of that, Paul had felt oppressed by it, as if his family's solid life was a trap he was being walked into. By me."

Her voice dropped to almost a whisper. "His parting words to me were that it was all just too boring."

Valentino stiffened beside her. "Boring?" he said, his voice soft and deliciously incredulous. And then indignant. "Boring?"

"Which I inferred meant *I* was boring. He certainly acted like it. I mean, near the end, he would barely look up from his phone."

Valentino snorted with an outrage on her behalf that Erin found quite sumptuous. "He wouldn't look up from his phone and he thought *you* were boring?"

"Well, I mean I know I'm not exactly a barrel of excitement. Look at me, a career accountant."

"Look at how you ski!"

"He wasn't a skier."

"You were with somebody who didn't share that passion with you? It *is* you."

It would be easy to just lap up his defense of her, but she felt driven to prove Paul might have had a point.

"I do have a kind of unusual attachment to my cat."

"He didn't like your Harvey," Valentino intoned with a sad shake of his head. "How could he not love the cat who saved you?"

Erin realized she had never shared Harvey's role in her life with Paul. A few hours in, this man already knew more about her secrets than Paul had in the entire length of their relationship.

Wasn't that telling her something?

As was the look on Valentino's face as he gazed at her. It felt as if she was being *seen* and, whatever Valentino saw, he did not seem to think it was boring. His hand left the cat's fur. It cupped her chin. His thumb scraped across her cheek. His eyes held hers.

"A man who could be bored with you is not even a man," he said firmly, his soft, accented voice as sensual as the touch of lips on the back of her neck.

She laughed a little nervously. Despite the

snowed-in-together confidences, there was a larger truth here they both needed to acknowledge.

"You don't even know me, Valentino."

Still, she didn't try to move away from his hand, and he looked stunned that she would suggest that!

"I do," he said fiercely. "No man could look into your eyes and not know you. And no man could look into your eyes and ever have a moment's boredom. Not unless there was something lacking in him."

"I'm not the kind that inspires great passions," she protested. But she was aware of how suddenly, and dangerously, she *wanted* to be that woman.

Valentino snorted, moved his hand from her cheek, tucked her hair behind her ear.

"Not inspire great passions?" he said, his hand still smoothing her hair. "A painter would die to paint you. The sun in that hair. That look on your face. A man could get lost in your eyes. He could dive into them as if they were a cool pond on a hot summer day. He could let what is in them fold over him, soothe him, hold him, heal the parts of him that are wounded."

Erin stared at him, her heart hammering so hard she thought it would break from her chest. This close, she could see the faint stubble beginning on his chin and cheeks. She was aware of the scent of him, as crisp, as exotic, as she imagined the land he came from would be.

Everything he was saying about her eyes held true for his own. Fringed with an incredible abundance of sooty lash, they were as rich as dark chocolate, melted. They held depth and compassion, and mystery. A mystery a woman could spend her whole life solving...

He dropped his hand from her hair and abruptly created some space between them on the sofa.

"I'm sorry." His voice was a scrape of pure gravel. "That was way too personal. I'm not generally—" he looked genuinely abashed "—given to poetry." Then his eyes found hers again and he sighed with a kind of surrender.

"But that is what your eyes do," he said softly. "They call out to the poet in a man."

Oh, God, something in her was absolutely melting. They'd had too much wine, obviously. Both of them. Too much wine, and the feeling of being safe inside, together, as the storm raged on, was creating a natural affinity between them.

Even knowing those things, even knowing what they were experiencing was akin to being shipwrecked on an island together, it felt as if she was being seen in a way she had not ever been seen before.

And she wanted, suddenly and urgently, to be a person she had never been before.

Not boring.

But the one Valentino had just seen. Fully a woman. A sensual woman who called to the painter in a man, and the poet.

She wanted to embrace the adventure of finding out who she really was, if there were hidden facets of herself that she had never discovered.

It felt as if maybe she never would discover those hidden things if she did not say *yes* to what was right in front of her, in this moment in time. She wanted, not to shrink away from the power he said she had, but to embrace it, to uncover it, to unleash it.

She wanted to get lost in his eyes and say *yes* to whatever hid in their dark, compelling depths. Empowered by what he had said, she reached out and traced that plump split in his lip. At that touch, her heart felt as if it had slumbered.

Not just now, but with Paul, through her entire life, a protective layer around it that fell away like a thin layer of ice tapped with a hammer.

Valentino went very still. His eyes were steady on her face, full of knowing, full of hunger. And then he opened his mouth ever so slightly, just enough to nibble the finger that explored his lip.

A kind of insanity overtook her. A delicious loss of mind. Years of careful control evaporated as if they had been a muddy puddle waiting for the heat of the sun. Years of feeling as if she knew exactly who she was vanished like a mirage in the desert.

This was who she really was.

This was who she was always meant to be.

She leaned into him. And she took his lips with her own. His hands came up and bracketed each side of her head, tangled in her hair. He pulled his mouth away from her and whispered endearments in her ear in another language, his words soft with the poetry of the heart.

Then his mouth found hers again. Urgent. Questing.

And Erin's world was changed for all time. Even as she took his lips, she knew whatever was happening, she could never, ever, go back to the way it had been—and she had been—before this moment.

"Love me," she whispered against his lips. In her tone, things she had never heard before. Urgency. Desperation. Hunger. "Please."

"How could I do anything but?" he whispered back.

CHAPTER SEVEN

VALENTINO PICKED UP ERIN, cradling her against his chest as he strode down the short hallway into the darkness of the bedroom. She wrapped her arms around the beautiful column of his neck. She did not consider herself a small woman, and her ex had consistently made her feel as if she came from the land of the giants.

Yet, in Valentino's arms, in the effortless way in which he had lifted her and now carried her, she felt light as a feather, exquisitely feminine and desirable. She felt cherished. She felt he was like a warrior who had found his way home to the maiden who had waited, her candle lit, believing he would come, even before she had known his name.

If they wanted light, the lamps would have to be lit. But she liked the room as it was, the atmosphere dimly lit and dreamlike.

He set her tenderly into the billowy embrace of a white down comforter. The bed was a beautiful, intricately carved antique that had come with her great-grandparents from Norway in the eighteen hundreds.

It felt right and good. That this bed that had been woven into generations of her family's love stories, was where she would come to know Valentino in every way possible for a woman to know a man.

He stood over her and as her eyes adjusted to the deep shadows, she saw that he was staring down at her with a gaze both tender and fierce. His hand moved to the buttons on his shirt.

He had forgotten his bandaged finger and so had she, and they both laughed, breathless with anticipation and delight, as she scrambled to kneeling and he came to the edge of the bed. She undid the buttons of the shirt one by one, her eyes never leaving his face.

When she was done, she got off the bed to stand before him. She peeled the plaid fabric off him, over his shoulders, caressing the naked skin beneath the shirt as it was revealed to her. Finally, she tugged each arm out of its sleeve. The shirt dropped from her fingers to the ground, leaving her to stare with stunning avarice at what she had unveiled.

Valentino was absolutely perfect. The

weak light from the gas lamps in the other room outlined the carved lines of his arms, powerful triceps and biceps, illuminated the broadness of his back, and spilled over the wideness of his shoulders. She had thought, because of his abundance of curls, that he might have a hairy chest, but he did not.

His skin was taut and golden, hair-free, molded to the perfect plain of a deep chest, the pebbles of his nipples, stretched over the slight rise of his ribs and the slender, hard curve of his belly.

She reached out tentatively and laid her hand, splayed, across his heart, and the sensual silk of his warm skin made her mouth go dry. She could feel the steady, strong beating of his heart under her fingertips.

He captured her hand, pulled it to his mouth, anointed the inside of her wrist with his lips and then tugged her yet closer to him.

His hands found the hem of her sweater and he hesitated.

His voice low, he asked, "Are you—?"

The sentence did not need finishing. Was she sure? Was she ready? She had never been more sure or more ready in her life.

Her tongue flicked to lips that suddenly felt dry and his eyes fastened there. She nodded.

There was nothing clumsy now, not even

with that bandage on his finger. He peeled the sweater up and over her head, her hair hissing from the static as her head popped free. He tossed the sweater away and smiled, taking in what he had revealed.

Slowly, tenderly, he smoothed her hair with the fingertips of his unbandaged hand, owning her in some way with that possessive gesture that made her mouth even drier, her breath even more ragged, her need even more acute.

Valentino looked at her, a man who could never get his fill, a man with eyes that would paint her. Words spilled from his lips, tender, soft, in a language so universal she did not need to know the words to appreciate their meaning.

He had come to worship at the altar of her femininity.

And she at the altar of his masculinity.

They had entered a dance as ancient and as sacred as the earth itself.

Little by little, slowly, with reverence, the rest of their clothes fell away, until it was just the two of them, at the beginning of time, exploring each other with wonder. With curiosity. With awe. Exploring the miracle and the marvel of a man and a woman.

Together.

Finally, when the urgency would not be denied any longer, they tumbled together deep into the embrace of the bed. Their bodies met, fused, entwined, melted. They climbed, and climbed, and climbed, exploring the jagged, endless precipices until finally they stood on the edge of a cliff.

And then, unhesitatingly, they leaped off.

Falling into the abyss of pure sensation. Joining the motes of cosmic dust that made up the stars. Joining what had always been; that place that did not acknowledge space or time.

Exhausted, content, they folded their arms around each other and, despite the storm that screamed under the eaves and at the windows, they slept the deep sleep of two people completely satiated.

Erin awoke in the morning to the sound of the storm still raging outside, as if it wanted to pick up the cabin, twirl it in the air and smash it down somewhere else on the mountain.

Her confidence in the sturdiness of the cabin strengthened her sense of contentment, her awareness of how her skin felt under the deep warmth of the down comforter and beneath the heat of Valentino's arm. It felt as if her whole body was tingling; the way it might feel going from a hot shower into a snowbank.

Valentino was on his side, one arm thrown possessively across the nakedness of her midriff, one leg pinning her legs as if, subconsciously, he had wanted to hold her to him, prevent her escape.

But she was a willing captive.

Erin turned her head to study him, aware that a smile amused her lips as she took in the wild corkscrew of messy curls, the stubble on his chin, the flawless perfection of skin that looked perpetually sun-kissed.

She waited for the sense of recrimination to come.

She had, after all, just spent the night—made wild love—to a complete stranger. And yet what she felt as she looked at Valentino was not recrimination. She did not feel that he was a stranger, but that she *knew* him as deeply and as completely as she had ever known another person.

She certainly did not feel any sense of shame. Or guilt.

But freedom.

Tenderness.

Delight.

She was marooned on a desert island with him and she had given herself, completely, to what the moment offered. And she was glad. It was very much like giving herself to the mountain when she skied.

It was a surrender. A great knowing that nature was, always, a more powerful force than you. But the surrender was such a joyous one, it became a dance.

Remembering what had passed between them last night, Erin was aware she felt grateful. She had almost given herself over to a life where this side of her—playful, passionate, curious, sensual—might have gone undiscovered.

Valentino stirred against her. His warm breath tickled her skin. She watched as the dark tangle of those lashes flicked open and revealed the melted-chocolate sensuality of his gaze.

She held her breath. Would he be the one who returned them to sanity? Would he be the one who pointed out that they were strangers? Who questioned if they had gone too fast, too far, too soon? Who asked if they were acting like survivors, exhilarated by the nectar of life, of being alive, without any care for tomorrow?

But when his gaze found her face, the drowsy smile—of welcome, of recognition—lit him from within.

His hands found her neck and tugged her to him, and he wished her good morning with a kiss that held back nothing.

Despite the fact they were in the tiniest of cabins—trapped here, really—with the storm still raging around them, it felt as if the whole world opened to her.

Embraced her.

Sighed for her.

This, then, was how it was meant to be.

Valentino was a man who had collected exhilarating experiences like other men might collect stamps.

He had skied some of the highest and most inaccessible peaks in the world. He had—over the objections of his security team and his family—embraced the sport of skydiving, throwing himself into the endless, vast blue of the sky. He had raced his horse at breakneck speeds over polo fields and along forest paths. He had a powerboat that, at optimum speed, would lift its nose and skim the water as if it were flying.

Valentino had experienced every thrill that being born to his station in life would allow.

And he was aware, now, as he watched Erin move through the kitchen with such grace, that every one of those things had been superficial compared to the exhilaration he felt, trapped by a snowstorm, and just being in the same room with her, sharing the same air as her.

Her hair was in a glorious mess and she had on a man's housecoat that would open every now and then to give him an enticing glimpse of long, long legs. There was a glow about her that could warm a man, as if he had come into a welcoming hearth on a cold day.

Which I have, Valentino told himself. The fire was spitting in the hearth, throwing heat. He had put on only the jeans from yesterday; his chest was bare. It was a kind of freedom to walk around in a state of half dress. And besides, just as he kept sneaking peeks at Erin's legs, she kept sneaking looks at him.

She leaned over and fed Harvey, murmuring to the cat, her fingers caressing his willing ears for a moment before she straightened.

Even that small gesture told Valentino who she was. Gentleness in her. A connection to living things. An ability to immerse herself in the simplicity and gifts of each moment.

And coinciding with those things, the incredible contrast of a passionate fire that burned white-hot within her.

Should I tell her who I am?

It felt as if he should. Right this moment,

before it went any further. She needed to know what she was getting herself into. She needed to have a choice.

But it would be the worst kind of distraction. It felt as if she already knew who he was. Better than anyone else, because she did not know about the titles, his position in life, his family. The mantle of royalty. For the first time in his life, Valentino felt *seen*.

He was not aware he had waited his entire life for that.

Until now. Until it happened.

She came and put coffee in front of him. His senses were so heightened that the aroma felt as if it could overwhelm him. But then that sensation receded as her hand found his hair and she combed it with her fingertips, tenderly, possessively. He turned his head and nipped at her hand.

Telling her the truth of who he was faded from his consciousness. It could wait. With the storm continuing outside—the snow so thick when they looked out the windows, they could not see across the clearing this morning—it felt as if there would be plenty of time for everything that needed to be said between them.

She laughed at his playful nip, and that glow intensified. She was alight with life.

"Breakfast," she said. She put a tiny heart-shaped cake down in front of him and sank into the chair beside his.

It was obviously a cake that had been made for Valentine's Day. It had a candle on it, shaped like a number one.

"What does the candle represent?" he asked.

"Me, alone on Valentine's Day," she said. Her laughter deepened, the light flowing out of her to embrace the whole room. And him.

"But now you're not," he teased her, pointing out the obvious. "So, should we throw the candle away?"

"No." She lit it. "It can represent firsts of all kinds. Make a wish before we blow out the candle."

"I wish," he whispered, "that this could last forever."

She was silent for a moment, her brow furrowed.

"What?"

"You're not supposed to tell anyone your wish. Then it doesn't come true."

He was taken aback by this North American superstition, but then realized how deeply he was under a spell. Because, obviously, it could not come true regardless. This could not last forever. Nothing could. The storm that rattled the cabin, that made him a grateful prisoner, would end.

"You make the wish, then," he said.

"I think you're only allowed one wish per cake."

"Too many rules," he decided, and the solemn moment evaporated, replaced by their laughter.

They blew out the candle together, their breaths mingling. She took up a knife she had brought over to the table with her.

Even he, with his inexperience at all things domestic, could see the knife was too large for the task.

"Hey, be careful with that thing," he said.

"Don't worry, I'm not about to trust you with it."

And then, to his surprise, instead of cutting the cake, she lowered that cleaver-like knife as if it were an ax. She chopped the cake into chunks instead of slices.

"I'm taking a lesson from your salad making," she told him.

"But I was going to start a cooking show," he said as he gazed at the mess of chocolate cake and icing on the plate.

She laughed. "Things don't have to be perfect to be...well, perfect."

She proved how true that was. Instead

of getting plates and forks, she picked up a chunk of the cake with her fingers and shifted herself onto his lap. He opened his mouth to her then licked the icing off her fingers. The massacred confection tasted of ambrosia, dreams and promises.

Following her lead, he dug his fingers into the rich darkness of the cake and fed it to her. And then he licked the icing off her lips.

Her turn. She took a chunk of that cake and pressed it into the nakedness of his chest.

Valentino groaned as she lowered her head and cleaned it off with her lips.

Soon there was cake everywhere and they were chasing each other around the small cabin, the cat hiding under the couch, miffed.

And then they were in the shower together.

And then back in bed.

He knew he had to tell her. But again, with the storm unabated outside, it felt as if time would expand endlessly and present him the perfect opportunity.

Obviously now, with the fires stoked in both of them, would be absolutely the wrong time.

Erin woke for the second time that day. She stretched like a cat, feeling luxurious, content, satiated. She was not sure she had ever felt this *full*.

She glanced at Valentino, sleeping on his back, his profile beautiful, his lashes as thick and sooty as a chimney brush, the whiskers darkening yet more on his face. She studied that yummy split in his full bottom lip. How could he seem so familiar already? How could it already seem as if she could not lead a life without him in it?

Crazy thoughts. This kind of thing, whether she wanted to acknowledge it or not, was a fling brought on by the intensity of circumstances, a powerful chemistry between a man and a woman stranded alone.

There was no point in contemplating the future. It would just ruin everything. For once in her life, she was going to give up her need to be in control, to figure out what happened next, to try to make her world safe and predictable.

For once in her life, Erin would do the unthinkable: go with the flow. Just see what happened next. Have no plan. She would immerse herself in the moment.

Her eyes drifted to the window. Still snowing. Still snowing hard. But she detected a difference in the ferocity of the storm, an abatement of the wind. Few people would attempt the mountain on a day like this, but she was so familiar with the slopes, she knew she could find the way down, effortlessly, to the ski village at the bottom of the mountain.

But she did not feel ready to let go. Not just yet.

His wish filled her. *I wish that this could last forever.*

Wrapping herself in the sheet, she got up and gave Valentino's bare skin a smack with her hand.

"Get up, lazybones. We can't sleep all day."

He opened his eyes and looked at her idly. With such frank appreciation, it made her skin tingle.

"I have awoken to a goddess," he murmured and then, pretending he was cranky, added, "Why can't we sleep all day?"

He wagged his eyebrows at her with wicked meaning that had nothing to do with sleep.

"We'll be awake all night if we sleep all day," she said.

He lifted that wicked eyebrow a little higher. "I can think of things to do if we're awake all night."

She smacked his bare skin again and he winced with exaggerated hurt.

"Get up. We should go outside and play. You told me about your island home. It's warm there all the time. How often do you have opportunities to play in the snow? Have you ever built a snowman? Had a snowball fight? Made a snow angel?"

"I have not done any of those things," he admitted.

"Then you must."

Before the spell is broken. Before the reality of nothing lasting forever sets in. Before the storm ends. A voice inside her insisted on reminding her, despite her intentions, of a future that loomed ahead, unknown.

"To tell you the truth, I'd rather—" he waggled his eyebrows at her.

"Stop it." She smacked him again. He held his arm with pretend hurt.

"Okay, okay. A snowman it is," he grumbled. "But this had better be good."

"Oh," she promised, "it will be."

And it was. Erin had never been with someone who had not experienced snow as a matter of course, as a life reality for four or five months of every year.

Valentino had skied, yes, but, just as she had guessed, he had never *played* in snow. They couldn't get a mitten over his bandaged hand, so she had carefully wrapped it in a scarf. And then, laughing, she'd had to unwrap it so he could get his jacket on.

She put Harvey's cushioned basket outside on the covered porch so that he could hear that she was near, and he settled into it contentedly.

The snow was still falling thickly, but the wind had stopped and it had warmed since yesterday. The ground cover was turning from the dry powder that everyone came here to ski, to the heavy, wet snow that was perfect for winter activities.

"First," she said, "Snowman Building 101."

"I think, in the interest of equal opportunities, we should build a snowwoman."

She scowled at him with feigned fierceness. "Are you going to be difficult?"

"Of course!"

"You take a little ball of snow—"

"Snowwomen don't have—"

"Stop it," she warned him, but she was snickering. "You take some snow and you shape it like this."

"That looks like a ball. I thought we had decided—"

"This is serious!" she scolded him. Of course, it was anything but.

She showed him how to put the ball in the snow and push it. Because the snow was so sticky and wet, it stuck to itself and the ball she was making got very large very quickly.

She had to get down on her knees and put her shoulder into it.

"A girl who likes big balls," he said approvingly, and she took a rest, scooped up some snow and tossed it at him. It hit him right in the face. He wiped it off with elaborate carefulness. And then he scooped up some snow and stalked toward her.

She got up from her snowball and took off running, aware that nothing was going to go as she'd planned, not even building a snowman. She gave herself over to the simple joy of being open to the moment and to whatever direction the energy between them turned itself in.

Erin did what had been demanded of her since the moment she'd met him. She gave up control.

Screaming with laughter, she tried to put distance between them, but the snow was just too deep. His legs were so much longer and more powerful.

He caught her easily, took her arm, spun her around. He pulled off her toque and smooshed his handful of snow into her hair. Then he tried to put the toque back on over it.

"That wasn't even a proper snowball," she said, wiggling away from him.

"You know, you seem preoccupied with the subject of balls."

She chortled. He threw back his head and laughed. The snowflakes danced around them, shimmering, as if they were the universal manifestation of the rhapsody unfolding between Erin and Valentino.

CHAPTER EIGHT

ERIN SCOOPED UP a handful of snow, smoothing it into a hard sphere with her hands. The cold sank through her mittens, making her fingertips tingle almost as much as they had as they'd explored the heated surface of Valentino's skin.

"Do you know what this is?" she asked him, trying for menace in her tone.

"Um, the item of your preoccupation?" he asked, grinning boyishly. When he smiled like that—carefree, mischievous, charming—it melted her.

"Wrong! Deadly missile."

She let fly. He ducked. The snowball whistled harmlessly by him. He straightened and the boyish expression was put away. He looked at her with pretend sternness—a look at least as sexy as his boyish one—and held up his scarf-wrapped hand.

"Do you think that's fair? Throwing things at a one-armed man?"

"All is fair…" she said, stopping herself just short of finishing the expression. *All is fair in love and war.*

She was certain that Valentino completed the phrase inside his head, just as she did. Because, suddenly, standing there, the snow collecting on their hats and coats and eyelashes, the world became very silent. And very, very still.

It felt as if a huge secret had just whispered itself out of the realm of mystery and into the realm of reality.

She broke the spell. She scooped up another handful of snow, and he took her cue, running, shouting taunts at her in two languages with a smattering of French thrown in for good measure. She let fly with the snowball. It hit him in the middle of his back. He fell as if he had been shot, and Erin dissolved into giggles. Then he rose and turned to her with yet another sexy look. This time, the warrior ready to win the battle.

He caught on to the art of the snowball fight very quickly, soon making deadly snowballs and aiming them at her with accuracy born of natural athleticism. The clearing soon echoed with their shouts, their taunts, their laughter.

They chased each other through the snow until they were breathless, panting for air. Until they could not run one more step.

Erin surrendered first, flopping into the snow on her back. He lay down his snow weapons and collapsed into the deep snow beside her, his shoulder just touching hers. She stuck out her tongue at the sky.

"Try this," she said. "Catch a snowflake."

He stuck out his tongue. She watched a fat snowflake fall on the sensual pink curve of his tongue and melt instantly.

He laughed, low in his throat, delighted. "It's like capturing a single bubble of champagne."

After they had rested for a while, catching snowflakes with their tongues, she rolled away from him then swept her hands up over her head in a wide arc, and then her feet.

"Snow angel," she told Valentino when he looked askance at her. She rose and stepped carefully out of the impression she had made to inspect it. He got up and stood beside her.

"That's quite remarkable."

And then he threw himself to the ground, on his back, and made a snow angel right beside hers, the wings touching. Having caught their breaths, their energy renewed, like children they raced around, throwing themselves in the snow, filling up the entire clearing with a veritable army of snow angels.

Sometime, while they were doing that, it registered with Erin, peripherally, that the snow had stopped. A watery light was trying to pierce the clouds around them.

Done with snow angels, Valentino was executing a new idea. Dragging his feet, he used them to draw a huge line through the snow, around almost the entire clearing, encircling the angels. After a moment, she saw that the line he was pounding out in the snow was taking on a heart shape.

She moved inside the heart and, with her feet, stamped out letters in the snow. Big letters, at least two feet high.

VALENTINO
ERIN

The sun burst through the clouds. The clearing turned into a fairy-tale land of white, the sun's glint making it blindingly bright, as if the snow had been threaded through with millions of sparking blue diamonds.

She could not stop the laughter when she was finished imprinting their names in the snow. With absolutely no planning on her part, the strangest thing had happened.

Erin O'Rourke was having the best Valentine's Day ever.

Valentino stood, his arm thrown around Erin's shoulder, looking at the valentine they had made. With the warmth of the sun on his face, the clearing sparkling with fresh snow, and her at his side, he wasn't sure if he had ever felt so happy.

A sound penetrated his happiness. The clearing was so silent that any noise would have seemed like a violation, but this one seemed particularly intrusive.

At first the sound was at a distance, but then there was no denying that the steady thrum was coming closer and closer.

Erin looked off in the direction the sound was coming from, puzzled.

"That's a helicopter," she said. "They wouldn't usually put it in the air unless there was an emergency." She went very still as she considered that. "I hope someone else wasn't caught in this storm. Shoot. I'm going to go get the sat device and check in. We might have to help with a rescue."

Just like that, she was running toward the cabin.

As she ran, the helicopter broke over the trees and hovered. A sinking feeling overcame Valentino. Not someone else caught in the storm.

Him.

The helicopter—the rescue—was for him.

With desolation in sharp contrast to his happiness of moments ago, he realized, just like that, it was over.

Foolishly, he thought, *I should have never spoken that wish—that this could last forever—out loud.*

His freedom was over.

And suddenly, guiltily, he saw he had enjoyed his freedom at her expense. She had no idea what was about to happen and he had no way to warn her. He watched as Erin froze on her way to the cabin, turned and shielded her eyes as the helicopter began to descend into the clearing.

For a moment, it was a complete whiteout as the wind generated by the blades kicked up a great cloud of white.

And then the cloud settled, the helicopter seesawed down, planted itself in the snow, and the engine was turned off. The blades slowed. Out of the corner of his eye, Valentino could see Erin, puzzled, coming back toward him.

The door of the chopper opened and Colonel Alisha Del Rento stepped out. Though she was not wearing a uniform, she was every inch the colonel in charge of his protection. And close behind her, the rest of his security team. They weren't wearing uniforms, either, but they might as well have been. They looked tense and ready to do battle with whatever they needed to.

"Your Highness," the colonel said just as Erin arrived at his side.

He felt Erin go very still. He turned and looked at her. Her baffled eyes went from him, to the colonel, to the rest of his men, and back again.

At first, she looked bewildered, but then something shuttered in those eyes that had been so open to him.

"'Your Highness'?" she said, her voice flat.

"Erin—"

She cast a glance at Alisha and leaned in close to him. "You lied to me," she said, fury in every clipped syllable she spat out.

His position suddenly felt indefensible, which drove him to want to defend it.

"Isn't finding out an ordinary man is a prince the best of surprises?" he asked her.

"No," she said without a moment's hesitation. "It isn't."

"I was going to tell you."

"Well, you know what they say about the road to hell." She stepped back from him.

"We have much to talk about," he said.

"That's your opinion. I don't feel we have anything to talk about."

Out of the corner of his eye, he registered the shock of Alisha and his security team at the tone Erin had used to address him.

Reasonably, he said, "Let's gather up our things and Harvey, and get on the helicopter. We can talk."

"I'm going to go down exactly the way I came in," she said. "I don't think we have anything to talk about, *Your Highness.*"

He heard something in her tone—particularly in the way she'd said *Your Highness*—that he was not sure he had ever heard before in his life.

Contempt.

The colonel had heard it, too, drawing in her breath with sharp and unmistakable disapproval.

Erin gave her a withering look.

"Don't go yet," she called, turning her back on him. "I have something for you."

Hope fluttered in him. Something for him. A memento. The wax number off the cake. Her phone number. Anything to cling to.

But when she strode out of the cabin moments later, she had two black-plastic bags. When Alisha tried to intercept her, she quelled her with a look.

She handed him the bags.

He peered in the first one. His clothes from yesterday. He looked in the other.

He realized, shocked, she had just handed him the garbage. Then she turned, nose in the air, and marched back to the cabin with as much dignity as the deep snow would allow. She did not look back. She scooped her cat out of his basket by the door, went in and slammed the door behind her with such force that the windows rattled in their panes.

Valentino found himself on the helicopter, lifting in that same cloud of snow. But as the cloud settled, before the nose of the helicopter was pointed downhill toward the resort, he saw it.

Their valentine.

Despite the clearing being so disturbed by the arrival of the helicopter, it was still there, even more spectacular from the air than it had been from the ground.

A lopsided heart encircled all those snow angels. And their names. His and hers, linked together. He cast a look at Alisha. She was staring down at the valentine. She glanced at him and then quickly away, her expression deliberately impenetrable.

But he had not a doubt that she and every other person on the helicopter knew that something had happened when he and Erin had been stranded in that cabin together.

The evidence was right there, printed in the snow.

He had forgotten, put aside, that he was not allowed the whims of ordinary men. He never had been. He had a role to play. An example to set. His was a life guarded against compromising situations. He was on duty all the time. He was not allowed slips. He was not allowed inappropriate liaisons. Not ever.

He waited for regret to come.

And found, in its place, defiance.

Erin stood with her back braced against the cabin door as if she were trying to hold out a band of marauders.

She waited until she could not hear the helicopter anymore before she moved away from the door. She thought she might cry, but she didn't. She was too angry to cry. She cleaned the cabin with a vengeance, doing dishes, putting bedding in the laundry, stuffing her backpack with her things.

"A prince?" she said to Harvey. "Family

business, indeed. No wonder I thought I recognized him. His ugly mug is at the grocery store checkout all the time."

If she was recalling it correctly, the paparazzi *loved* Valentino.

He's not ugly, a voice inside her insisted on protesting.

"Huh," she answered out loud. "Ugly is as ugly does."

Valentino was one of those men—just like her father—skilled in the art of seduction. All of it—the ineptness, the poetry—had probably been an elaborate act to get her into bed. And she had fallen for it! No, not just fallen! Hurled herself into it!

She felt angry, with Valentino and herself, and the anger was much better than feeling sorry for herself. It felt powerful. And passionate.

That passion—and the feeling of practically vibrating with energy—made her realize she was not even the same woman that she had been less than twenty-four hours ago.

Then she had been a *victim,* retreating from the world to lick her wounds, to feel sorry for herself about being dumped so unfairly by a man she had invested two years of her life in.

She didn't feel like that at all right now.

The truth was, she probably had Valentino

to thank for this passionate, powerful side of her rising to the surface.

Harvey was hiding under the couch, eyeing her warily, not at all used to this kind of energy crackling off her.

Finally, bedding in the dryer and cottage looking for all the world the way it had always looked—as if nothing exciting or unexpected had happened there—she was ready to go.

She strapped on the baby carrier, stuffed her cat inside it, pulled on her coat, her toque, her gloves, her backpack.

She closed the door behind her.

Was she going to be able to come back here? Or would this place—that had always been her sanctuary—be haunted now?

The ghosts of his smile, his touch, his eyes on her, taking up residence here and never leaving?

She gave herself a shake, turned away, got her skis ready.

The snow wasn't the feathery powder everyone came here for. It was heavy, wet. The kind that was perfect for making the snowman they had not made. Still, even with the snow so challenging, she attacked the downward slope. Threw herself into it.

The passion translated to the way she skied. She could feel it. She embraced the intensity and singleness of focus that mountain required.

Once she got to the village, she made her way to her apartment and dropped off her things. She was stunned that it was only early afternoon. It felt as if years had gone by. In fact, it was still Valentine's Day.

Rather than sit around her apartment sulking, ruminating, going over every detail of the events that had just unfolded, Erin decided to go to work. It was her hidey-hole, after all. She popped Harvey back in his carrier and headed across the resort, enduring the smiles of people who thought she was carrying a baby.

"I thought you weren't coming in today," her office mate, Kelly, said, looking up with surprise when Erin came through the door.

Erin noticed that Kelly's desk sported a vase with at least a dozen red roses.

"I changed my mind," she said, trying to slide through to her office.

"I assumed you and Paul had something romantic planned," Kelly said, shamelessly probing. Her eyes slid to Erin's ring finger, hopefully.

Erin pulled back her shoulders and lifted her chin.

"Paul and I are no longer a couple," she said.

She wondered why she had dreaded this moment. Why she had thought *her* failure would be, humiliatingly, on public display.

Because she didn't feel like that at all.

She felt free. And strong.

She felt like a woman who had heard a man say to her, his tone as touching as a caress, *No man could look into your eyes and not know you. And no man could look into your eyes and ever have a moment's boredom. Not unless there was something lacking in him.*

"I'm so sorry," Kelly said. "Perhaps it's just a spat?"

Erin lifted a shoulder, not prepared to go into the details with her workmate. She found the refuge of her office and shut the door. She took Harvey out of the carrier. He went gratefully under her desk and curled up right on top of her feet.

That was how easy it was to get back to normal. With the cat purring steadily at her feet, soon she was immersed in the world she loved. A world of numbers and formulas. When done correctly, there were no surprises.

Surprises. It triggered a memory of Valentino's voice. In her mind's eye, Erin saw him lift that glass of wine to her and offer a toast.

To surprises.

Is this what her life was to be like now?

Was she going to constantly be remembering a man she had spent so little time with?

Oh, but that time!

She shook it off.

Erin had just succeeded at immersing herself in that soothing world of work when her office door suddenly burst open. No knock.

Kelly, nearly lost behind a huge arrangement of flowers, said breathlessly, "See, I told you it was just a spat."

But Erin stared at the flowers, her mouth open, knowing this kind of extravagant arrangement was just not the sort of thing Paul would ever spend money on.

"I think its birds-of-paradise," Kelly said, setting them down and handing her a card. She stepped back to gaze admiringly at them. "And some kind of exotic lily. I don't think I've seen that before."

A tantalizing fragrance tickled Erin's nostrils.

"So beautiful!" Kelly declared, reaching out and touching the white, waxy petal of one of the lilies. She waited for Erin to say something, but Erin was stunned into absolute silence.

"Where do you get flowers like that at this time of year? They aren't from Berkley's Flowers. In fact, there's no tag on them at all. Just that card I handed you. Believe me, I looked! The delivery man wasn't what you'd expect. For some reason, he reminded me of a soldier. He said he'd wait for your reply. He had quite the yummy accent."

"My reply?" Erin managed.

"I think Paul's outdone himself. Open the card!"

If there had been any doubt who the flowers were from, the fact that a man who looked like a soldier and had a yummy accent was waiting in the front office, erased it in Erin's mind. She thought of the men and the woman who had tumbled out of that helicopter ready to rescue their prince.

Definitely soldiers.

Erin remembered his description of his land: the colorful flowers everywhere.

But even he could not have had flowers brought from there this quickly. Still, even without Kelly telling her, Erin knew that the small florist shop in the village could not have produced anything like this bouquet.

Of course, money would be no object for him. He'd probably had some staff member order the flowers and then sent a helicopter to pick them up.

The card was probably a brush-off. *Thanks*

for a memorable time. But then, why would the messenger be waiting for a reply?

"Are you going to open the card?" Kelly asked anxiously. She turned and peered out the office door. "Yes, he's still there. I think Paul wants to set up something special. I bet he's going for forgiveness!"

Erin's fingers fumbled with the creamy envelope. She slid out a thick card and stared at it.

Kelly was absolutely correct. On one count, anyway.

She had the message right.

She just had the wrong man.

CHAPTER NINE

ERIN HELD THE creamy-white card. Who on earth had stationery like this on hand, particularly when they were traveling on a vacation? Silly to be seduced by the feel of paper, but it was so thick and rich. Possibly handmade. It was also ever so subtly embossed. The royal crest rose out of the paper and she explored the soft ridges with her fingertips.

That was who had stationery like this. A prince.

The card was handwritten, which made it harder to dismiss. His writing was strong, masculine, spiky.

Please forgive me. Give me an opportunity to explain. Would you come to my suite for dinner tonight?

It was signed *Valentino.*
That newfound sense of herself and her

strength faltered. She felt weak with wanting to see him. Just like that, she could imagine his eyes on her eyes, his hands exploring her skin, his lips claiming hers. It made her feel as without strength as a newborn kitten.

But that helpless sense of weakness was just one more reason to say no. What would be the point of seeing him, of hearing his explanation? Where could such a liaison as the one they had shared possibly go?

There was no future in it.

Does everything have to have a future in it? A voice inside her whined. *Does everything have to have a point?*

She thought of the lovely intimacies they had shared: bandaging his finger, eating together, being in his arms, waking up beside him, exploring every inch of him, chasing him through the snow.

She could feel the blood rising in her cheeks. The desire to see him again was unbelievably strong.

She read the final line.

Please bring Harvey.

For some reason that tested her resolve even more than remembering Valentino's lips on hers. He had *heard* her. He understood that she tried to keep the cat with her as much as possible; he understood what Harvey meant to her. Nobody had ever included Harvey before.

Paul had barely tolerated the aging cat and the feeling had been mutual. He had *hated* her attachment to her beloved pet. "Weird," he had cuttingly pronounced it.

But before she gave in to all this temptation, swirling around her like a storm trying to suck her into its vortex, Erin took a black felt marker out of her desk drawer and wrote *NO!!* across the entire invitation.

Under Kelly's horrified eyes, she stuffed it back in the envelope and passed it to her.

"Give this to the man who is waiting."

The great prince couldn't even come himself? Obviously, he had used his resources, and very rapidly, too, to sort out where she worked at the resort.

No. Their worlds were too far apart. If this was that important to him, he could have come himself. He had lied to her already. She had made love to an imposter.

Not that she had to explain her refusal to herself or to anyone else. *No*, according to a self-help book she was reading, was a complete sentence.

"But—" Kelly said. Her voice drifted away

when she saw the look on Erin's face. She turned, reluctantly, and left the office, shutting the door quietly behind her.

Valentino put his phone down and went to the window. From his penthouse suite, he looked out over the Touch-the-Clouds resort. The quaint mountain village was snow-covered, bustling with the after-storm activity of colorful parka-clad skiers. The mountain cradled the resort in its bowl.

And tucked away in those mountains, a secret place, where it felt as if he had left his heart. He had just spoken to Angelica.

She had cried with relief when he'd told her he was not going to ask her to marry him. She had been so grateful but worried, too, knowing the brunt of the breakup would be borne by him.

He sighed and rolled his shoulders. He had told her, truthfully, that he was grateful, and prepared to pay the price. Whatever it might be.

There was no mistaking the sense of freedom. Of shaking off the harness he had worn since the day he was born. He was scheduled to leave tomorrow, and he felt he had to get home as soon as possible. The whole betrothal celebration must be canceled before any more work went into the preparations. Even at this point, it would probably be akin to trying to stop a runaway train. But it had to be done.

Valentino returned his attention to the card his guard had returned to him while he was on the phone.

He took a deep breath and slipped it out of the unsealed envelope.

He stared at it, incredulous.

Erin, in thick, black felt marker, had scrawled *NO* across the surface in two-inch-high letters, adding two exclamation points just to make sure he got it.

The feeling of incredulity died. He was not sure why he was smiling. He should be insulted. But just like that bag of garbage she had handed him, he didn't feel insulted.

Intrigued. A tiny bit tickled. Now that she *knew* who he was, she was not treating him any differently than she would any other guy who had hurt her feelings.

He thought of them in her bed together and admitted to himself that it went a little further than hurt feelings.

Where was it going, then? An apology and a goodbye on good terms?

But why? He was free of the matrimonial expectations that had been placed on him.

Why couldn't he—they—see where it all could go?

The truth was, it had been many years since anyone had said no to him. Still, he'd obviously gotten it wrong. You didn't, apparently, beg for forgiveness by way of royal summons.

He had so much to learn.

And he realized he was hoping Erin would be his teacher. But first he had to get her to see him again!

Erin looked at the clock. Time to go home. But why go home? All she would do was think about things she could not change. The only thing that mattered to her—Harvey—was here with her. She could stay in the office, order supper and keep working.

She could be having dinner with a prince. But, no, she'd be sharing a ham sandwich from the staff cafeteria with Harvey...

A knock came on the door. Kelly, no doubt, to remind her it was quitting time. But Kelly came in, slid the door shut and leaned on it. Was she trembling?

"Kelly?"

Kelly opened her eyes. They were wide with shock. "*He's* out there."

"Who is out there?" Erin asked, trying to

keep her voice calm. Of course, she already knew what kind of man would elicit this kind of reaction. Of course, in his world, he would not take no for an answer. Why hadn't she anticipated this and gone into hiding?

"The Prince of—" Kelly glanced at the card she held in shaking hands "—Lorenzo del Toro. I've seen him in magazines. But nothing could prepare me for him in real life." She sighed with so much feeling that Erin feared she might faint.

But then she pulled herself together. *"You know him."* This was said with faint accusation, as if Erin had willingly withheld a secret—that Kelly's survival depended upon—from her.

"Casually," Erin said then felt her cheeks burn. She knew full well why she had not gone into hiding. Because part of her—even with all the evidence that such things were naïve and foolish—hoped.

"He's asked me to announce him," Kelly said and giggled. "I feel as if I should have a trumpet. Toot-doodle-loo! Announcing—"

"Just let him in," Erin interrupted her.

Kelly opened the door wide and called, "You've been announced," then dissolved into girlish giggles as Valentino brushed by her, giving her an indulgent look.

Erin folded her arms over her chest and did not stand.

Kelly looked from one to the other and, sensing the tension in the room, scuttled out. Valentino closed the door behind her.

"What do you want?"

"I wanted to tell you I'm nearly completely recovered from my injury. See?" He held up a finger. Her first-aid attempts had been replaced with a very neat and tidy—not to mention, small—bandage.

He seemed—adorably—like he didn't quite know what to do now that he found himself there. For a man who commanded a nation, and stood so strongly in himself, it was seductively charming that he was off balance, unsure.

She had to fight an urge to get up and go look at his finger. To take it, and maybe to touch it with her lips… Erin shook off those thoughts, absolutely appalled with herself. She glared at him.

He cleared his throat, dropped his hand into his pocket.

"I wanted to tell you how sorry I am. Since you won't have dinner with me, I have brought the message to you. I should have told you who I was. I never meant for you to be shocked like that."

The very sound of his voice—deep, tender, genuine—weakened her. As did his eyes on her face.

Pleading.

A prince was pleading with her, Erin O'Rourke, for understanding. She felt a lump in her throat. He elicited so much feeling from her. It was dangerous. It was a feebleness.

"All right," she managed to say. "Apology accepted. Your conscience can be clear. You can go now."

A touch of a smile tickled the line of his lips. She ordered herself not to look at that bottom one.

"Is something funny?" she asked.

"It's just no one talks to me like that." He made no move to go. "Please, come have dinner with me tonight. It's my last day here. I fly out tomorrow. I have urgent matters to deal with."

"I get it," she said. "*Princely* duties call you. This will shock you, but I have a life and obligations, too. I can't just drop everything because you have summoned me."

This was so patently untrue that if she was Pinocchio her nose would grow about six feet right now.

"You have a previous engagement," Valentino said. He looked so crestfallen, she felt that dangerous softness for him inside her intensify. If she was not careful, she would be like Kelly, nearly fainting from his nearness.

"But it's been nice meeting you," she said coolly.

"Erin," Valentino said, his voice hoarse, "I just, for once in my life, wanted to be a man like any other. I wanted to be liked for myself and myself alone.

"Whether you forgive me or not, that is the gift you have given me."

She digested that. She felt her position compromised. She hadn't thought of it from his perspective. She hadn't thought how hard it would be to never be sure if someone liked you for you or because you were a member of a royal family.

She had not thought how someone, who had never had it, might long for normal.

"All right," she said, "I accept your apology. And I forgive you. Now, you can go."

He still didn't move. His look of relief was so genuine. "Would you have dinner with me tonight? Please. Perhaps your other engagement can wait, since I'm leaving first thing in the morning? I feel there are things we need to discuss."

"What kind of things?"

"The future."

One thing being an only child of warring parents had taught her was that hope—especially hope that love could win—was the most dangerous thing.

Love?

The intensity of what they had experienced wasn't love. It was a survivor's euphoria of some sort. The isolation, the storm, had led to impulse. A sense of embracing the moment. Infatuation. Passion.

She was going to say no to his dinner invitation. She really was. It would take all of her strength, every single bit of it, and still, the rational part of her knew there was only one answer.

There was no future for an ordinary, common Canadian girl with a prince.

But just as she was forming the word—how could a one-syllable word prove so difficult to get out—Harvey roused himself, stretched and came out from under her desk. He peered around the corner in the direction of Valentino.

The cat was mostly deaf. He was partly blind. He was antisocial.

And yet, somehow—perhaps by that thing called instinct that was so well-honed in the animal kingdom—he knew exactly who was there.

He shot across her office floor with more speed than Erin had seen in him in years. He wound himself around Valentino's legs, "talking" loudly.

Valentino laughed and picked up the cat. He lifted Harvey over his head and then brought him down to his face and planted a kiss on the tip of the cat's nose. He then hugged him into his chest and held him there.

It was the way somebody might handle a baby. She didn't want to think about Valentino with babies.

Babies. That's what she had wanted with Paul. In fact, she had wanted it so badly, it had taken away her discernment, her ability to tell the difference between fantasy and reality. And, of course, there was the fact Valentino was a prince. There would never be any babies with him.

And yet, seeing him with the cat, there it was nonetheless. A longing so powerful it nearly took her breath away.

"Are you going to come for dinner with me tonight, my old warrior?" he asked. He looked to Erin for the answer.

Baby thoughts should have put her defenses up higher. Instead, whatever was left of them crumbled. "Okay," she said, "we'll come."

The fact she was having unexpected longings for babies should provide ample protection against temptation to have another tumble with him. Having a baby was a serious enough business without adding the complication of a prince!

Besides, he was probably surrounded by a veritable army of people at all times. No wonder he had enjoyed his time on the mountain. It seemed to Erin that would be a perfectly awful way to live.

An hour later, standing in front of her mirror in her own apartment, she knew she had been put under a spell and that it was wearing off. Because, really? The dress she had on was terrible. Never mind that she had loved it when she had bought it to attend an awards dinner her father was being honored at. It was the fanciest thing she owned—jade green that matched her eyes, off-the-shoulder, short and sassy. Now, it felt as if she was trying too hard. Way too hard.

She had been in the presidential suite, which the prince and his entourage were inhabiting, only once. The resort had reserved it for a retirement party for the CEO of the company. The suite took up the entire top floor of the Northern Lights Hotel and was posh in a way she hadn't even known existed.

Of course, you wore your best dress for that. To have dinner with a prince.

But then she recalled what he'd said about the gift she had given him of feeling normal.

Gratefully, with a sense of relief, Erin slid off the dress that suddenly made her feel like a child pretending to be a grown-up and threw on a pair of casual stretch jeans and a button-down shirt. She put on a hint of makeup and tucked her hair up into a messy bun.

Then she remembered his fingers taking the pins from that bun—it seemed like a lifetime ago—and the veritable avalanche that had unleashed. She took her hair back down and, before she could overthink it too much, tousled it with her fingers. She pulled on her jacket, picked up Harvey and zipped him inside, and headed out into the Touch-the-Clouds complex.

It was a beautiful star-studded evening and she was aware of it as if the night was alive around her.

But that wasn't quite it.

It wasn't the night that was alive. *She* was alive—tingling with a kind of nervous anticipation—in a way she had not been in a long, long time. If ever.

When she knocked on the door of his suite, she wasn't quite sure what to expect. Staff?

What did she say? *I'm here to see the prince. I'm here to play Cinderella to his Prince Charming.*

But Valentino opened the door himself, welcomed her by kissing her, with some formality, on each cheek. The cat popped his head out and Valentino took him from her jacket, good-naturedly kissed both his cheeks, too—just to let her know she wasn't getting special treatment?—and then set him on the floor.

Harvey, blind as he was, ambled across the space and found the most expensive-looking, silk-covered chair in the opulent main living area that was right off the front door. He gathered himself and leaped with surprising prowess into it then curled into a contented ball.

"Apparently he considers himself suited to such a palatial lifestyle," Erin said. The suite was as she remembered; a gorgeous space where you were afraid to touch things. Evidently, Harvey did not share her intimidation.

"May I take your coat?"

She shrugged out of it and was instantly aware that Valentino did not normally take coats, because he stood there not quite knowing what to do with it.

She gently retrieved it from him, opened the coat cupboard and hung it.

"You look lovely," Valentino said.

It made her glad she had not worn the dress. He, too, was dressed casually in pressed jeans and a V-necked sweater over a collared shirt. He looked very much the ordinary guy— except for those luxurious dark curls and a handsomeness that would never allow him to be ordinary!

"Humph," she said, regarding him thoughtfully. "I thought, now that your secret is out, you might have had a prince outfit on."

He glanced down at himself. "What, exactly, would you imagine a *prince outfit* to be?"

"At the very least, a hat with a shiny brim, like army officers wear. I would think some medals. One of those wide ribbon things across your chest."

He was smiling. She enjoyed making him smile.

"You don't know any more about princes than I know about igloos."

"Or delivering babies," she reminded him. She snapped her fingers. "You should at least have a sword!"

He laughed, as she had hoped he would, and that tension she'd been holding since she had said yes to this invitation dissolved a little bit. This was her Valentino. The one she had chased through a snow-covered meadow.

Shared a bed with.

Not that she wanted to go there. But how was it not going to go there? The tension returned and intensified yet more as he led her through to the dining room. Like the main living area, this room was traditional and opulent. The long, polished, walnut table was set for two with beautiful china, both settings at one end. One at the head and one beside it. Valentino surprised her by holding out the head chair to her. Surely, that was his place at the table?

He took the other chair and reached for the bottle of wine that was sitting in a silver bucket.

"Note, it has already had the cork removed," he said with a grin. "And as an extra precaution, I'm decanting it. According to the sommelier, that lets any sediment drift to the bottom."

The grin, so familiar, tried to ease something in her, but the fact he had a sommelier at his disposal worked against that ease. Now that she was thinking about it, she could hear noises in the kitchen, which, if she recalled from the other time she had been here, was behind that swinging door. Delicious smells were wafting out of it. Unless she missed her guess, someone was preparing dinner for them.

Well, what had she thought? That he was going to order a pizza?

"I considered impressing you by uncorking it with a sword—"

Valentino, that man whom—in a complete break from her normal buttoned-down personality—Erin had loved shamelessly and spontaneously, was really a prince. And that prince wanted to impress her?

What strange fairy-tale world was this that she found herself in?

CHAPTER TEN

VALENTINO GRINNED AT Erin. It made him, dangerously, *her* Valentino and not a world figure of considerable fame and fortune.

"As I said, I considered uncorking the wine with a sword, but I couldn't find one on such short notice. Someone neglected to pack my ceremonial one."

That, all kidding aside, meant two things: someone packed for him and he actually *had* a ceremonial sword.

"All things considered, that is probably a good thing," she said solemnly and lifted the glass he had poured for her. "I propose a toast."

He lifted his glass.

To surprises, she thought. But out loud she said, "To keeping all your digits."

He wiggled his newly bandaged finger at her. And just like that, the laughter bubbled up between them as effervescent as the wine.

Her discomfort eased, but then came back as the swinging door to the kitchen opened and a white-uniformed staff member came through. A royal crest had been tastefully embroidered in gold thread on the breast of his uniform. He was bearing platters of food.

"Your Highness," he said. "Miss."

As he set down the food, did he slide her a look that was ever so faintly disapproving? She shot Valentino a glance to see if he had noticed, but he did not appear to have. Surely, she was being overly sensitive and had imagined it?

"May I bring you anything else, sir?"

"No, Milo, thank you."

Did Milo give her another look before sliding silently from the room?

"I wanted you to have a taste of my country," Valentino said and served them both from the platters.

She took the snowy-white napkin from beside her setting and put it on her lap. She regarded the array of cutlery with a bit of hesitation. Her lifestyle had rarely required she knew which fork to use! In this new setting, the passionate, carefree, confident woman Valentino had coaxed to the surface mere hours ago seemed to be fading with alarming quickness.

Erin watched how Valentino addressed the feast that had been prepared for them, and she did what he did. She was aware that he was as much at home in this world of amazing food, impeccable manners and culinary rituals as she was a foreigner in it.

Her disquiet lessened when he shifted his chair over closer to hers. He plucked a tiny tomato out of a glorious salad with his fork.

He held the fork to her lips. "Try this."

Her lips closed over his fork and flavors exploded in her mouth, possibly made more intense by his closeness, by his fork being in her mouth.

"Delicious?" he asked her.

"Unbelievable." Did that kitchen door squeak open and then shut again? "Somehow I don't think you picked that up at the Snowbound Groceteria."

He laughed. "It was developed by our palace horticulturalist. Its name translates to Tiny Tornado Tomato. We export them around the world now, to upscale markets."

"You travel with your own food?"

"My chef would never chance being able to find the quality or specialty ingredients he likes locally, I'm afraid. When we travel, he brings everything with him. He's snobby that way."

"Isn't it illegal to transport food into another country?" she asked. "My father once got off a plane in New Zealand with an apple they had given him on the flight—and he was charged a fine."

He contemplated that. "I have no idea, but I'm sure we would not do anything illegal. Probably we obtain permits or special permissions."

We. Meaning not him. She realized Valentino simply did not attend to the details of everyday life.

He moved on, making her taste the olives separately. They, too, were a specialty product of his kingdom, developed by the palace horticulturist. Taking great pride in the culinary accomplishments of his island home, Valentino explained each item on the menu to her. Every savory piece of food was evocative of a warm and colorful place.

Still, horticulturalists? Chefs preparing food? Sommeliers? Wait staff? People who quietly looked after permits and entry requirements? Protection staff?

"You must have been laughing when I called that salad at the cabin Mediterranean salad," she said. "Tasting this, it so obviously was not. You must have laughed about quite a bit of that meal. Steak that fell on the floor—"

"Licked by a cat," he told her, his eyes crinkling with merriment.

If she could just look at his eyes, maybe she could believe... "What? You never told me that part!"

"I protected you from it," he said, pleased.

"Oh." A prince protecting her. It stole words really.

"It was one of the best meals I have ever eaten," he said softly. "I would not change one thing about it. Except maybe the cork in the wine."

When the main meal was finished, Milo came out and prepared dessert at the table, two wedges of creamy cheesecake that he spooned a cherry topping onto. And then, with great flourish, he produced a torch, lit it and set it to the cherries. A blue flame danced over them briefly and died.

Milo looked so pleased with himself that Erin almost forgave him the subtle signs of disapproval he was giving off, especially now that Valentino had moved his chair so close to hers.

Valentino waited until Milo had left the room before he took his fork and fed her the stunningly delicious dessert.

She had a sudden memory of eating cake

off his chest and felt embarrassed. She would have never done that, if she had known.

She would have probably never done any of it, if she had known.

Valentino seemed to sense her uncertainty. He picked up her hand and turned it, kissing the inside of her wrist.

"Let's talk about the future," he suggested, his voice low and sultry.

The future? Cinderella and Prince Charming belonged in fairy tales. As much as it felt like she had been dropped into one, she had to keep in mind that in real life, worlds that were so different collided, they didn't converge.

"What future?" she asked.

"I want you to come to Lorenzo del Toro. With me. Let me show it to you."

For a moment, she could almost feel the warmth on her skin, smell the scents. But she had to keep one foot in reality! She had to.

"Obviously, I can't. I can't just drop everything. I have a job."

"Surely, you get holidays?" he said persuasively. "Isn't the ski season nearly over?"

"We have a shoulder season." Not enough of one to bring them out of the red, but still, it kept the resort open and paid basic bills.

His eyes slid to her shoulders in a way that nearly melted her.

"I have a life," she insisted, hoping he would not ask for examples because, at the moment, a life—one without him in it—seemed particularly dreary.

"A cat," she added weakly.

"Harvey can come with you."

He really did not know anything about how real people lived!

"You don't just board a plane with your cat," she told him.

He looked confused, as if that had never occurred to him. But then he laughed. "Oh. Do you think I'm asking you to take a commercial flight?"

"Aren't you?"

"Of course not. We have a private plane. I would send it for you."

Erin was dumbfounded. *He would send a plane for her?* She had grown up with plenty of international traveling, but she had never been on a private jet.

She closed her eyes and let the seduction of the whole thing sweep over her. A vacation in an exotic place. With incredible food. Sunshine. Discovery. A private jet. An intriguing, gorgeous, sexy man.

Milo slid back through the door and stood silently until Valentino acknowledged him with a look that clearly said *Not now.*

Milo, however, was not to be deterred. "Your Highness…"

The formal address, the man's deference to Valentino, reminded Erin, again, how far apart their worlds really were. How she didn't really know Valentino at all.

He was not just the playful man who had given himself over to loving her, to playing with her in the snow…

But he was holding out an opportunity for her to get to know him better and on so many different levels. They had shared her world. Now he was inviting her to explore his.

She could feel herself leaning toward it…

Milo spoke. "Sir, the palace has just announced your engagement to Princess Angelica of Sorrento. I wanted to be the first to congratulate you."

Valentino gave the man a stunned look and then dismissed him quickly with an impatient wave of his hand.

Erin froze and let the words sink in. She felt as though she had been slapped. In fact, she fought back the tears rising in her eyes.

Instead of letting him know her distress, she got up slowly, feeling as if she were in a dream. Even knowing better, even having grown up with her father, *still* she had fallen for Valentino's charm. Still, she had believed he'd wanted to show her his world.

"So," she said, tossing down the napkin, "apparently there are two things you neglected to tell me. One, that you're a prince. And two, you're a prince in a committed relationship."

His dark eyes were liquid. He looked at least as distressed as she felt. But she squeezed any sympathy she wanted to feel for him out of her heart. She tilted her chin proudly.

"Let me explain." His voice, his beautiful voice, was low and pleading.

"You had plenty of opportunity to explain," she snapped. "Any time up at the cabin might have been good. Before we were intimate comes to mind."

"Erin—"

"But maybe you don't have to follow the same rules as the rest of the world? Is that it?"

"That's not it. At all. If you would just listen to me—"

"To your explanation? Maybe you'd like to run this by your royal speech writer, but it's pretty hard to explain an engagement to someone else to the woman you have just invited to share time with you." Erin could hear an unnatural and very unflattering shrillness in her voice. She told herself to be quiet. But she couldn't. The words just kept spilling out of her, furious, outraged.

"When were you going to tell me that part? About the princess being your fiancée? Once I was there? When you were hiding me away somewhere like a tawdry little secret?"

Her mother's exact words to her father. *Your tawdry little secrets.*

"How were you going to keep your betrothed, Princess Whatever-Her-Name-Is, from knowing about me? Or is that kind of thing acceptable in your country?"

"Erin, it's not like that. I promise you, it's not like that." He was getting up, easing toward her, gently, like one would ease toward a skittish colt that wanted nothing more than to bolt.

She *wanted* to hear it. She wanted his promises. She wanted his words to smooth it over so that it all made sense.

That's how stupid she was!

"No, I don't want to hear it," she lied, holding up her hand to him in the universal gesture of *Stop right there, buddy.* "I've heard enough explanations, thank you. You can put all the finery around it that you want. You can have your staff and your plane and your exotic food and people who light it on fire for you. It doesn't change the truth."

"The truth?" he asked.

"You, Your Royal Highness, are a complete ass."

Valentino watched, shocked, as Erin stormed from the room. The cat yowled in protest when she picked it up and a moment later the door slammed behind them.

He was tempted to go after her.

Not that he had much experience in these things, but instinct told him there were certain times that you would be taking your life in your hands trying to talk to a woman.

Besides, as he sank back down at the table, he allowed himself to feel the full insult of it. Erin *knew* him. She had to know him. It felt as if she was the only person who had ever truly seen him.

And she was so quick to believe the worst of him.

An *ass*?

No one had ever spoken to him like that before. He had never been called such an insulting name in such a scathing tone.

His indignation faded. Valentino felt a horrible sense of defeat. He resigned himself to the possibility that whatever had happened between them on that mountain was a moment of magic, somehow separate from time and space. It could not, it seemed, be recaptured here on earth.

Perhaps it had served its purpose, giving him the impetus to set Angelica free. For that dazzling moment in time, on the mountain with Erin, he had believed a different life waited for him, but now he was not so sure.

It was obvious to him that someone in his inner circle had reported his involvement with Erin went further than them stranded together in a snowstorm. That valentine stamped in the snow had been a dead giveaway. The delivery of the dinner invitation to Erin's office this afternoon had probably cemented conclusions.

He had been reported, by someone, to his mother, the queen. Possibly, the palace even knew he was entertaining Erin tonight. Probably, Milo had been instructed to make sure that Erin went home and had been given the ammunition to do that.

His family were pulling out all the stops. They were trying to drive him back into the fold, trying to force his hand, with the engagement announcement coming early.

It didn't really matter who had reported him. There was no point chastising them, or Milo, the server who had made the announcement in front of Erin. His staff were loyal to him. But in the end, everyone in the kingdom, including himself, answered the commander in chief, who was his mother. His staff had probably all been ordered to do whatever they could to nip the romance with the Canadian girl in the bud.

Before it had a chance to become an embarrassment.

Or, more important, before it had a chance to persuade him to put his own happiness ahead of his sworn duty.

He had to return to his island immediately. He would announce his breakup with Angelica to his mother personally. There were going to be repercussions, but still, he had to make it clear that certain elements of his life would belong to him alone.

He looked at the remains of the dinner in front of him, his appetite gone. In fact, he felt quite ill.

Milo came through the door. He noticed the empty place and, for just a second, a look of carefully controlled sympathy crossed his face.

"Can I bring you anything else, sir?" he asked.

"No, thank you."

It was everything that Valentino had grown up with: a civil exchange. Emotion was swept under the carpet; the show must go on. Dignity and decorum. The public perception came first and foremost. Always. Control, and discipline, were everything.

He resisted, just barely, an urge to pick up a plate and throw it at the wall.

CHAPTER ELEVEN

ERIN WOKE UP the next morning to the sound of a helicopter lifting in the distance. The steady whomp of the blades slicing the air intensified the pounding in her head. She felt, for all the world, as if she'd had too much to drink, when she was pretty sure she had only had a few sips of that cork-free wine.

She told herself to ignore the noise, but she couldn't. She knew, in her heart, what the sound meant.

Valentino was leaving.

The helicopter would take him to wherever his private jet was parked. Did you park a jet? Was that the proper terminology? Moor it? Who cared? Stupid to waste time wondering about such things.

He was engaged.

Still, if she got up and went to her living room window, she could probably catch a glimpse of the aircraft that carried him. Away from her.

Forever.

Had she really thought, when he'd invited her for dinner, that something could ever come of it? Besides a fling?

She was hardly the kind of girl who inspired grand passions. She was not the kind of girl a prince would choose.

With those thoughts running through her head, Erin refused to let herself run to that window. Her pillow was damp with tears. The hangover she was feeling was an emotional one. Harvey, ever sensitive to her mood, was curled up, purring on the pillow right by her ear. It was reminiscent of the days of the childhood that she had been so determined to leave behind her.

Is that what she had clung to in her relationship with Paul? The fact that emotional turmoil had been happily absent?

But, come to think of it, strong emotion of any sort had been absent. Was that any way to conduct a romance?

Not that what she had experienced with Valentino could qualify as a romance. A tryst, maybe. *A tawdry little secret.*

The prince was engaged.

It was shocking news, never mind that he

had seemed as taken aback by Milo's announcement as she herself had been. The fact that Valentino had been romancing Erin—carrying on with her—when he was committed to another woman was despicable. Unforgivable.

It was just like her father. So sure of his charms. Gullible women falling all over themselves to be with him. Probably, women who didn't have a very good sense of themselves in the first place, so wanted to bask in the reflection of his glory.

"Yuck," she said out loud. The sounds of the helicopter had long since faded. She finally got up. As tempting as it was to call in sick, she knew herself too well. Moping helped nothing.

So she scrubbed her face and got herself and Harvey ready to go to work.

An hour later, she was crossing the village square, the snow crunching under her feet. The main floor of the building she worked in housed a minimarket—the one she had teased Valentino about *not* shopping at—and she had to pass right by it to get to her office.

Any hope she had that there was some mistake about Valentino's engagement—that the surprise on his face meant something for the future he had talked about for them—was blown to smithereens.

The tabloids were out on a display rack in front of the building this morning. There were three different ones, but all had a variation of the same front-page headline and story.

Fairytale Romance:
Prince and Princess to Marry!

Someday My Prince Will Come:
Royal Engagement Announced!

Royal Romance:
Prince Valentino Proposes to
Princess Angelica!

Erin was not quite sure how Valentino had managed a proposal since he'd been having dinner with her at the very time his engagement had been announced.

In his world, she thought, miffed, he probably had staff to look after the bothersome little details of an engagement. The Royal Proposer.

Naturally, she hoped Valentino's betrothed was what he deserved, cold and unfeeling. A horrible person. She hoped she had blotchy skin. But, no, Erin herself was the only one with blotchy skin this morning. The pictures that accompanied the headlines did not show an ugly princess. The furthest thing from it, actually.

Angelica of Sorrento was, naturally—and unfairly—gorgeous, right off the pages of what the heroine of any a fairy tale should look like. She had an abundance of wild, dark curls, an amazing complexion, soft, dark eyes, eyelashes as thick as Valentino's own.

They would make beautiful, curly-headed, golden-complexioned babies together.

In one of the pictures, the happy couple had their heads together, nearly touching, laughing. The caption said it had been taken at a polo match the previous summer.

Of course! A polo match! Erin was surprised the prince wasn't playing in it! Who went to polo matches? Rich people. Sophisticated people. Who had jets.

And who had paramours tucked away in the far corners of the globe.

In another of the pictures, they were both on horses, riding a quiet forest trail, each looking completely comfortable in jodhpurs and riding helmets. Looking completely comfortable with each other. Looking exactly what they were: the most privileged, pampered people on the planet.

The third picture showed Angelica at the top of a curved marble staircase in a gorgeous gown, long gloves, a tasteful tiara. Every inch the princess. Valentino waited at the bottom of the stairs. Look at that! Dressed *exactly* like a prince, including the sword.

Erin, shocked at the level of her own anger, ungraciously hoped he would manage to chop off a finger while uncorking the wedding champagne.

She itched to buy one of the papers—to feed her desire to know everything there was to know about him—the jerk—but recognized it would do nothing but cause her more pain. So, with difficulty, she refused the urge.

Kelly was already in the office, at her desk. Any hope Erin had that she might have missed the tabloid headlines was lost when she stuffed one of the very papers Erin had just looked at in her desk drawer and gave Erin a look loaded with empathy.

Erin felt, horribly, like the unwanted sympathy might make her burst into tears. Hopefully, she had cried them all out last night. Hopefully, she did not have a single tear left to waste on Prince Valentino!

She hustled into her office, released Harvey from the carrier, and immersed herself in the world that had always been engrossing for her. She wished it brought more comfort. The storm yesterday had come too late. The season was now nearly over. If the snow held, they might have another month. Ticket sales were down nearly twenty-five percent over last year. She had heard several of the concession owners saying they were not having a good year, either.

She had nearly managed to block out everything but the numbers in front of her, when the office door squeaked open.

"Do you want to know the latest?" Kelly asked.

Erin, unfortunately, could not keep her curiosity at bay. She nodded reluctantly.

Kelly came across the floor to her desk and handed Erin her phone. It was open on the web edition of *Rags and Riches,* one of the most notorious of the tabloids.

Erin was stunned to see there was a new headline.

Royal Splitsville:
Prince Calls Off Engagement!

She read the story with an uneasy greediness to know what was going on in Valentino's life.

Only hours after it was announced, Prince Valentino of the island Kingdom of Lorenzo del Toro has called off his engagement to Princess Angelica of the neighboring island of Sorrento.

The prince himself is tight-lipped about the unfolding situation, but the royal family has issued a statement that they have every hope the couple, who have known each other since childhood, will reconcile. They ask for privacy at this time.

Neither the Sorrento royals nor the princess has released a statement, but sources close to her say she is devastated by the stunning callousness the prince has showed in breaking their engagement, which is now, humiliatingly, among the shortest in history.

After that, over the next few days, no matter how hard she tried, Erin couldn't avoid news of him, even if she wanted to.

The headlines had turned nasty. *Happily Never After!* one read.

News turned out to be a loosely applied term because there was really no news, not that that stopped the paparazzi feeding frenzy. Where there was no news, there was no lack of conjecture, no shortage of "sources close to" willing to give statements and expose the depths of heartbreak and misery the princess was experiencing.

Very powerful telephoto lenses, drones and helicopters were capturing pictures of both the prince and princess from a distance and through windows. The criteria for the photos seemed to be to catch Valentino looking grim-faced and cold—villainous and evil—and Angelica looking tear-stained, bewildered and broken—the fragile victim.

If Erin wasn't so angry—*spurned* was probably the correct word—she would have almost felt sorry for Valentino and the hounding he was enduring.

She did feel sorry for Angelica. Was she responsible, in some way, for that stranger's now so very publicly exposed misery? Responsible in the same way that those women her father had taken up with had been responsible for her mother's pain?

In her weaker moments, Erin asked a different question. What if she wasn't just the other woman? Wasn't one of many in a long string? What if Valentino had felt something in the time they had spent together that had made him realize he wanted more—that there could be more?

What if what had happened between them wasn't a sham at all, but was the most real thing that had ever happened to either of them?

What if what he had felt with her at the cabin was the reason for his broken engagement?

But those thoughts would be followed so quickly with *Who are you kidding? Who do you think you are?*

It was so confusing it made her head hurt. Erin felt as if she had a chronic headache. And then the worst possible thing happened.

A week into the tabloid feeding frenzy, Kelly came into her office and closed the curtains that covered the window that overlooked the village square.

"Don't look out there." Kelly passed Erin her phone.

Stunned, Erin saw a fuzzy picture of herself, looking quite frumpy, crossing the very resort square that Kelly had just closed the curtains on.

Under the terrible picture were the words *Prince's Secret Woman?*

Erin was dumbfounded. "How on earth?" she whispered.

"I think any number of people, both here on the mountain, and among his staff, know that the two of you were trapped together overnight. There was plenty of chatter about it in the main office. Then I heard lots of whispers around the resort that you'd had dinner with him. I'm sure that tidbits like these are worth a fortune to these kinds of rags."

She, Erin O'Rourke, girl least likely to create any kind of fuss, ever, was fueling this kind of gossip?

She thought of that toast she had made. *To surprises.* It occurred to her a toast like that required clarification: *Good* surprises.

"They're outside the window, aren't they?"

Kelly went and peeked out the closed curtains. "I'm afraid so. Clamoring, like sharks circling in anticipation of a gut bucket."

Did she have to be that graphic? Erin handed Kelly back her phone. Her coworker swiped to another screen and handed it silently back. There was an even more terrible picture of her, with Harvey creating a bulge under her jacket.

The papers had made the same mistake Valentino had made on their first meeting. The headline blared *Prince's Paramour Pregnant?*

Erin passed Kelly the phone back. "Don't show me any more," she pleaded. Her own phone started to buzz.

"I hope they don't have your number," Kelly said.

But it was Paul's name that came up. Considering, at least before she had met Valentino, that she had longed for this call—and the announcement he had come to his senses, that she was clearly the best thing that had ever happened to him—she looked at it with reluctance. Now? Really?

She hesitated and then, from long habit—she'd always been so thrilled when he'd called her, found time for her—she answered.

"Paul," she said. She heard the total lack of enthusiasm in her own voice. She had been going to marry this man! Why would that make her feel like a loser? She could have had a nice unremarkable life, without any of the current chaos unfolding around her.

She was aware, just like that, she wouldn't take him back, no matter what. Was the current price she was paying worth that realization? She thought it probably was. And then some.

"And I thought you weren't exciting!" Paul said jovially. "A prince?"

He sounded oddly titillated, certainly as interested in her as he had ever been. He obviously was eager to have the inside scoop.

Erin was shocked by what came out of her mouth. "You're an ass, too."

Erin hung up the phone. Kelly giggled, shocked.

Erin's phone started to ring again, almost right away. The number was unknown. She stared at her phone in horror then quickly powered it off.

"Can you get a hold of Ricky for me?" she asked Kelly. "He's probably working the Lonesome lift today. Tell him I need to get up to the cabin, without anyone knowing."

"Done," Kelly said and then looked at her with such grave sympathy. "Oh, Erin, really? You? You are the least likely person to get caught up in something like this."

Almost the exact same message she had just gotten from Paul!

She was getting the same message, over and over, for one simple reason. It was true.

The ache she'd been nursing for days intensified until it felt as if her head were going to explode.

Ricky arrived within the hour and smuggled Erin and Harvey out a back door of her office building and onto a snowmobile. Even the drive up the mountain was good for her head. The further they got away from the chaos, and the more into the quiet sanctuary of high places, the better she felt.

By the time Ricky dropped her off at the

cabin, with a sat device, her headache had almost completely cleared.

"Don't use it unless it's an emergency," he said. "We don't know yet who's yakking to the press. But I'll tell you this—I wouldn't want to be them when I find out who it is."

"I wouldn't want to be them, either," Erin said, taking in the menacing look on his craggy old face. He looked very pleased with that assessment and, with a final wave, roared off back the way they had come.

"Family comes in so many different ways, doesn't it, Harvey?"

Just a short while ago, she had resigned herself to this. To her family being the people she worked with. Harvey.

It now, sadly, felt as if it would not be enough to fill the space left in the wake of Valentino.

The sound of the snowmobile engine grew more and more distant, and Erin regarded the cabin and the clearing. She could almost hear her and Valentino's laughter.

She needed to clean the slate, literally. After she deposited Harvey inside the door, she went and kicked snow over where she had stamped their names until the clearing was scrubbed clean. Well, except for the angels.

She left the angels. She felt as if she needed all the help she could get.

She entered the cabin with a bit of trepidation. So much had unfolded here! She was going to have days to do nothing but relive memories and be with her tangled thoughts.

The best antidote to the thoughts that haunted her—the main one being *Who do you think you are?*—was to keep busy.

In the daytime, with Harvey happy in his baby carrier, she snowshoed and cross-country skied until she fell into bed at night exhausted.

The ache inside her dulled as she filled moments with busyness that shut off the chatter in her mind. The wood needed to be restocked, kindling always needed replenishing. She found some sandpaper and stripped down the kitchen set, ready for repainting. She had books and she had crossword puzzles.

On her third day in exile, Ricky arrived with groceries and an envelope.

"Are things settling down?" she asked.

"More vultures than ever camped out looking for you," he said.

"They're not letting it go?" It was easy to believe, up here without the internet or TV, papers or radio, that everything could be normal again.

"Um, I think there have been some new developments. I think Kelly put a newspaper in that envelope for you."

"Oh, dear," Erin said without enthusiasm.

"There's been this strange side benefit," Ricky said brightly, "the resort has been rediscovered."

"Rediscovered?"

"We couldn't buy this kind of publicity. The phone is ringing off the hook at the office. The website crashed. Twice. We're taking bookings for three years away. We've sold more season passes in the last week for next year than we did all this year."

This was what she needed to cling to, Erin thought as Ricky drove away. That there was sometimes a bigger picture. That good could come from bad.

She took her time getting to the envelope. Finally, she opened it.

She was stunned by what she saw.

It was a newspaper, folded in two. The half of the headline she could read.

Happily-Ever-

The photo, also folded in two, showed half of a happy couple. The part of the picture Erin could see was of a joyous Princess Angelica.

Her fingers trembled. After all the ker-fuffle, the engagement had been foregone. They had gone straight to the wedding. Angelica was an unbelievably beautiful bride. The dress was like something out of a dream. The white handmade lace of the veil against her dark curls was the picture of a perfect fairy-tale ending.

Angelica was the kind of girl who had happy endings. She had been born to them. Erin, the one who was not that kind of girl, couldn't bring herself, not just yet, to unfold that paper to see the other half of the happy couple.

CHAPTER TWELVE

VALENTINO STARED AT the photo of Angelica, radiating joy in her bridal finery. She had sent it to his phone yesterday, before releasing it to the press.

He recognized the groom only vaguely. A member of her protection team, a wholesome-looking young man who clearly would lay down his life for his new wife.

Valentino sighed. He had done his best to protect her. But, no, in the end, she wasn't having it.

She had called beforehand to tell him what she intended to do. He'd tried to talk her out of it and she had laughed.

"Oh, Valentino. I know you mean well, but you're being terribly old-fashioned. I don't need you to carry this burden for me, so that the press can have you as their villain."

"But now they'll make you the villain," he

warned her, aching for the misery she was leaving herself open to.

When she'd answered, her voice was strong. "It doesn't matter. I know who I am. It has nothing to do with the stories they tell. You know that. This is my choice to make. It is my right to choose." And then, softly, adding, "Antonio will protect me."

It was someone else's job to protect her. He hadn't realized how seriously he took that self-appointed responsibility until she'd said that, and he'd felt relief wash over him.

One less thing in his world that he was responsible for.

And so, against the express wishes of her parents, and her people, Angelica had run away—taking the beautiful dress and the heirloom veil that was probably intended for her marriage to Valentino—and married the man she'd chosen.

And then she had freed him, Valentino, by publicly releasing a few photos of the event. In those photos, she and her new husband's eyes shone with light, almost blinding, as they looked at each other.

There were going to be repercussions, and many of them, and Angelica and her new husband's faces said that love was worth it. That love made them strong enough for whatever came next.

So far, the paparazzi were indulging the pure romance of a runaway princess bride. But they were clamoring at Valentino's door more than ever. They wanted their story. They wanted to capture him sad and angry and betrayed. They wanted the spurious kind of elements to the story that sold papers.

This was the press: hero to zero and back again, in the blink of an eye.

Of course, his thoughts turned to Erin. He longed for her. Had she seen this? Would it change everything between them? Was there hope? For them? Was there a way, just as there had been a way for Angelica and Antonio?

Could he even, in good conscience, ask her that? He had planned to, that night everything had blown up in his face and she had declared him an *ass*. He had specifically invited her to see if they could discuss the future.

That had been impulsive. He had still been riding the wave of intensity that their time together had created.

Crazy. They barely knew each other. She had made it clear she didn't want to change that. She had made it clear what she thought of him.

Had she seen the news of Angelica's marriage? Surely, it would change her mind? What would he do if it did? If she contacted him?

He would ask her, again, to come here. To see if she could fit into this world, or more important, if she would want to.

But the days went by and there was no word from Erin. Could he blame her? Those horrible pictures that had been printed of her, the headlines, had no doubt given her a taste of the viciousness she might leave herself open to if she chose to pursue a relationship with him.

Valentino fought the urge to be the one to bridge the gap between them. No. If he really cared about her, he would not invite her into this life but protect her from it.

For the next few days, his course chosen, he threw himself into his duties. He did his best to forget her. They had been together in that cottage for less than twenty-four hours. How could he possibly be so changed by that? So obsessed with her? He longed for Erin with an ache that was physical.

He was barely eating and he wasn't sleeping. It might not be the best time to make a decision, but it was in that vulnerable state that he arrived at his conclusion.

This was his truth.

He had been born to power. He was a disciplined man. He had nearly always done what his station required of him.

So he was shocked by this awareness, this unfolding truth, that when it came to Erin, he was powerless. He *had* to see her. If she was not going to come to him, he had to go to her. He could not fight it.

There were pieces to set in place, naturally, so that the press would not be hot on his trail. He and Erin needed privacy. He would arrange a leaked story. Maybe even a decoy to send them in the wrong direction.

While he followed the direction his heart was leading him in.

It was nearly dark when Erin came back through the clearing. She had cut it close, but she was glad. She had snowshoed all day. She was exhausted. Hopefully, that meant tonight she would fall into bed too tired to even think *This is the bed we shared.*

She stopped short and frowned.

There was a light on in the cottage. The golden light from the gas lamps inside spilled out the windows and across the snow, warmly welcoming, like a painting on a Christmas card. She shrugged it off. She must have left them on this morning, but usually she was not careless with the gas lights. On the other hand, nothing about her seemed "usual" right now. Admittedly, she had been distracted.

As she got closer, she realized there was also a faint whiff of woodsmoke in the air. Surely that would not still be there from this morning's fire?

She felt a bit annoyed. Had some skiers or other mountain enthusiasts found her little sanctuary and made themselves at home? These mountain cabins were always left unlocked in case they were needed as emergency shelters, and she didn't begrudge anyone that, but she didn't feel up to company, either.

She had another thought. Maybe it was her father, taking a break from gallivanting around the globe, an aging playboy. Maybe, like the rest of the world, he was curious about her notoriety.

She felt as if she didn't have the energy to deal with him right now, either.

Making as much noise as possible, so much so that Harvey gave a little mewl of reprimand from inside his carrier, she took off the snowshoes, slammed them together and clumped up the steps to the porch. The door opened just as she put her hand to the latch.

She braced herself, but nothing could have prepared her for—

Valentino.

"Hello," he said softly. His voice was like a caress. His eyes were like a homecoming. She wanted nothing more than to fly into his arms.

But—

"Aren't you married?" she snapped.

"Married? Me?" He tilted his head at her. "How long have you been hiding up here?"

She didn't like it that he knew she was *hiding.* From the world. From her pain. From the insecurities that had, unfortunately, followed her.

Who do you think you are?

"Someone sent me the paper."

He quirked an eyebrow at her. Something was wrong with his eyebrows. They were white at the tips, and curling, as if he had cleaned a spider web with them. It was distracting.

"Of me? Married?" he asked, innocent, incredulous.

What kind of world was this he lived in? A celebrity world, obviously. One she could never belong in. Wouldn't want to! Engaged one day. Not engaged the next. Married one day…

Did those vows not mean anything to anyone anymore?

She stormed by him.

The paper lay where she had tossed it on the kitchen table. It was untouched, still folded. She grabbed it and thrust it at him, crossed her arms over her chest, waited for his *explanation*. Oh, how he loved to explain things!

Instead, he looked down at the paper. He looked up at her and had the nerve to smile.

"Sometimes," he said, "you just have to look at the world from a different angle."

He turned the paper over.

She saw the headline completed:

After!

And she saw the photo—the one she had been avoiding but could not quite bring herself to burn—of the groom looking adoringly at his new bride, Princess Angelica.

And that groom was not Valentino.

Her head shot up. She stared at him. Her mouth opened and then closed. She could feel tears filming her eyes.

"Come," he said, helping her out of her jacket, taking Harvey from her. "Sit down. I've made you hot chocolate."

She sat, stunned, while *the prince* brought her hot chocolate, sank beside her on the couch, watched her with that familiar warmth in his eyes. His eyebrows were still distracting.

She was dreaming, naturally. She took a sip of the hot chocolate while she contemplated his eyebrows. Scorched. Surely, in a dream, the hot chocolate would be perfect? And his eyebrows wouldn't look like that.

"Did you have some kind of incident lighting the stove?"

He cocked his head at her and looked a little sheepish. "And the lamps. How do you know that?"

The prince looking sheepish was too adorable to resist. She reached up and touched his eyebrows. "Your eyebrows have turned to ash."

"Better than ass," he said, straight-faced.

She giggled.

"I watched you light the stove and the lamps several times. I might have had the sequence wrong. There was kind of a poof and a flash of fire and light. It was a little more excitement than I anticipated doing such a simple task."

The truth was that everything he did made simple things exciting. But she needed to remember there was a very thin line between excitement and disaster. That *poof* he described was about three seconds away from a cabin burned to the ground.

"Are you ready to let me explain? Ass that I am?"

She nodded. Her heart, that organ she had thought was dead inside her, was living again, thudding a tattoo inside her chest. "Yes, please tell me why you are here. What's going on. Why you didn't marry Angelica."

"Angelica and I have known each other since we were children. It was expected of us that we would marry. Love, of course, does not have anything to do with these kinds of arrangements in families like ours."

A man like Valentino—so passionate, so alive—condemned to a loveless life? It made her feel furious at the system he was bound to.

"To my shame, now, I didn't feel my marriage had to have love. She's beautiful. I respected her. And liked her. We're good friends, which I suppose is a love of sorts."

A love of sorts, yes, Erin thought, but not the kind you married. And yet, wasn't that *exactly* what she herself had been going to do? Marry Paul without passion?

"I actually felt as if I'd done fairly well

in the arranged marriage department," Valentino continued. "Both kingdoms were in a frenzy of preparation for the engagement party."

Again, the parallel—she, too, had thought she had done fairly well in her relationship with Paul.

"But then she told me she didn't love me."

Just as Paul had told her. Not that he didn't love her, not exactly, but that something was missing.

"And I knew by the way she said it, that she already loved someone else. She said, of course, she would go through with our marriage. It was her duty. What she'd been born to.

"That's when I came to Touch-the-Clouds. I needed to think. There is something that cuts the legs out from under a man to hear a woman that you care for talk about marrying you as if it will be a trip to the gallows.

"I think I already knew in my heart what had to be done. But would I have had the courage to do it? Before I met you? Before I found out what I would be asking both her and I to miss? Maybe not. But, believe me, the first thing I did after I got down from the cabin that day after the storm was phone Angelica to tell her she was free.

"And then I was free. To ask you to dinner."

Erin was struck by the truth of it: they had both been on course to make a tremendous mistake. They had both willingly accepted less than they'd deserved from life.

She owed Paul a debt of gratitude that he had somehow seen that something was missing.

Valentino owed Angelica that same debt of gratitude that she had freed him.

They both owed it to the universe to embrace this second chance they had been given to get it right.

"Oh, Valentino," Erin whispered. "I called you an ass. I didn't even give you a chance."

"Well, given that my engagement was unexpectedly announced—equally surprising to me as to you—I can hardly blame you. Though I did at first. I blamed you. I was hurt.

"I thought you, of all people, should know who I was. My family—my mother, the queen—had gotten wind that I was with you. She rushed the announcement, thinking it would force my hand, force me back into the fold. She counted on me to be who I have always been. A man who put duty first.

"But when I left here, and I wasn't that man anymore, I couldn't put anything first, before what I had felt for you. So, I called it off. I tried to make it seem as if it had been my decision, hoping it would protect Angelica.

"Unfortunately, even having lived with the media all my life, I could not have predicted the ensuing circus."

He smiled wryly. "Angelica let me know, in no uncertain terms, she did not need my protection. And that she would make her own choices.

"Which were to be true to herself and show the entire world she was not afraid to marry the man that she loved."

"I've been a complete idiot," Erin said softly. And not just about getting angry with him, jumping to conclusions, but about accepting so much less from life than it wanted to give her.

"Yes, you have been," he teased her.

She slugged him softly on the arm and he pretended hurt. "At least I didn't blow up my own eyebrows."

They laughed and the laughter made something inside Erin sing back to life. She realized she had not laughed since he had left.

"What now?" she asked him. "Where do we go from here?"

"Before," Valentino told her, "I wanted you

to come to my kingdom. I wanted to see if we could have a future."

She registered the *before*. Her heart fell. She had, it seemed, missed her chance.

"But now?" she said. "Why are you here if I have thrown away my chance?"

"Thrown it away?" he asked, astounded. "That's not it, at all."

"Then what is *it*?"

"Traveling to the kingdom right now is out. The press are on me like hounds on the fox. If you showed up now, they would never leave us alone. We would have drones buzzing us every time we tried to step out. I couldn't ask you into that, and I needed to escape it.

"And then I thought, *I know the perfect place to escape*."

"That's why you're here," she said. "To escape."

"Why are you so resistant to the truth?" he asked her softly.

"Which is?"

"Erin, I want to be with you. I was dying without you. Yes, I want to escape. I want to get lost in your eyes. I want to dive into them as if they were a cool pond on a hot summer day. I want to let what I see in them fold over me and soothe me, to heal all the parts of me that are wounded.

"I want to see where this all can go. I want to spend a week up here, intensely with you, and nothing else. How many places in the world would allow such an experience?"

That was true. She had never seen the cabin quite like that. A sanctuary. A love nest, hidden from the rest of the world.

"I want to see if the universe brought me to a ski hill in a storm so that I could change my destiny," Valentino told her softly. "So that I could know love instead of duty."

Love?

It seemed so wrong. It seemed too soon. It seemed so right. It seemed as if the rules of time were silly structures, not intended for them.

Destiny.

That is what this felt like. Destiny.

"Is it wrong to want to do so without the surprise of a drone shot of our most private moments being splattered all over the front pages? I admit I have sent the paparazzi on a bit of a wild-goose chase, worthy of their own devious devices, so that I could have time with you. Just you."

Erin carefully set down her hot chocolate.

And then she leaped into his lap, twined her arms around his neck and took his lips with her own. Homecoming.

"I plan to fit into your world," he informed her between kisses.

Didn't he know he already did? Wasn't it obvious?

"I brought books with me. So we don't get bored."

"I don't think there's much chance we are going to get bored," Erin told him. Still, if he'd brought books, she was hoping for the *Kama Sutra*.

Or maybe they could lie in bed and read Elizabeth Barrett Browning to each other.

"How do I love thee? Let me count the ways..."

"How to Build an Igloo," he announced, pleased.

CHAPTER THIRTEEN

As IT TURNED OUT, Valentino discovered building an igloo, aside from needing perfect snow, required several elements that the book failed to mention.

For amateurs, building an igloo required a good sense of humor. It required puzzle-building ability. It required tenacity. Most of all, it required that he and Erin to work as a team.

If you wanted to get to know someone, he decided, building an igloo was nearly the perfect way to do that.

But that activity—and all else they did from cooking simple meals to making the bed together—was overshadowed by the awareness of each other that crowded out nearly everything else. Everything was complicated by it...and made better by it. His life had taken on a light that shone more brilliantly than the sun on snow around them.

Her laughter filled him.

Her touch healed him.

Her intelligence awed him.

Her strength complemented his strength.

Erin and Valentino had somehow happened on an activity that unveiled to them how, despite so many cultural differences, they were incredibly compatible.

And despite the fact they exhausted themselves on their project, they barely slept. Talking deep into the night, often falling asleep with the next word dying on their lips.

And yet they woke energetic, filled with excitement for another day spent together. Valentino had never felt so exquisitely and intensely connected to another human being in his entire life.

It filled a part of him that Valentino had not been aware was empty.

Finally, three days and six collapsed, abandoned, restarted, rethought, reconfigured igloos later, they stood staring, awed, at their completed project.

The polished snow blocks that formed the dome got their strength only from leaning on each other. There was no additional supporting structure.

There was a lesson about life here, Valentino thought.

"It's supposed to support the weight of a man standing on the roof, if we did it correctly," he announced.

Erin grinned impishly at him and crossed her fingers.

Like an ice climber, he scaled the rounded wall. On the top of it, he pulled himself to standing. It was a gorgeous, spring-come-early kind of day. He surveyed the clearing that had become his world: the cabin, smoke chugging out the chimney; the clearing still filled with the melting outlines of snow angels; closer, the cat in a basket they had brought for him, belly to the sun, paws pointed at the air, indifferent to their accomplishments.

Valentino crouched and held out his hand to Erin.

She giggled—that carefree, breathless sound he had come to live for—and took his hand despite the fact she was protesting.

"Does the book say anything about it supporting the weight of two people?"

"Let's live dangerously," he suggested and pulled her up beside him on the dome. It was a perilous balance on the slippery curved surface, but they clung to each other, as interlocked as the snow blocks.

Isn't that exactly what they were doing?

Living dangerously? Challenging every limitation others—and themselves—had tried to put on them?

The structure—their salute, really, to forging their own way in a world that wanted to tell them what to do—held.

He kissed her and let go of her hand. Erin slid on her bottom off the roof and he followed her, the crystal-clear air of the clearing ringing with their laughter.

He gathered supplies they had brought—a blanket, a candle, a thermos of tea—and crawled through the ice tunnel that led to the interior of their snow structure.

Given how bright it was outside, it was fearsomely dark in there. He spread the blanket and lit the candle. Erin wiggled in, the cat in her jacket.

It was tinier than they had first envisioned, but that meant the candle they had brought in, plus their body warmth, heated the space, as the book had promised it would. There was just enough room to shrug out of their jackets.

"It's tight in here," Erin said.

"Cozy," he corrected her.

"Here's to cozy." Erin unscrewed the lid from the thermos, put it to her lips and then passed it to him.

He took a sip and offered his own toast. What had become *their* toast.

"Here's to surprises."

Four full days with her and she was still surprising him in the most delightful ways. He still loved his lips touching places her lips touched, like the rim of the thermos. Still lived for intimacy between them, small touches. Still was awed by the growing comfort, the heated looks, the moments of quiet contentment.

Harvey, on her lap, seemed quite crabby about the whole experiment. He glared back and forth between them, as if to say, *Uh, we have a perfectly good cabin...what nonsense is this?*

Nonsense of the best sort, Valentino thought.

And yet getting to know her better was an agony, too. Because, every day, his feeling that he could not live in a world without her intensified.

But this snowbound world was perfect. Here they could be private. And playful. Completely themselves.

Could he really expose her to the deep scrutiny that she would encounter in his world, a world completely alien to her?

Could what they had discovered about each other here stand up to the very unusual stresses of his life? At this moment, flushed with triumph and accomplishment, all his doubts fell away. In this moment, it felt as if what they had could stand up to anything.

"You have showed me your world," he told her.

She smiled. "That's not exactly true," she said. "You have showed *me* my world. Opened my eyes to it. Showed me a way of looking at it, and a way of being in it, that I did not have four days ago."

She reached out and touched his cheek. Her eyes on his face held an expression that was everything a man could ever hope for.

Valentino felt *seen*.

He slipped his own hand up to cover hers, slid her fingers to his lips and tasted the now familiar taste of her.

If two people could use nothing more than their intention, their intelligence, their willingness to learn, to build a structure that could hold their weight out of something as flimsy, as insubstantial, as snow, couldn't they do anything?

"Come to my world," he whispered. "Let me show it to you. Everything will seem new. Please say yes."

She looked at him deeply.

Valentino was aware that everything Erin

knew was here. This was her world. Over these days together, he had discovered, as she'd talked about her life, how safe she had made it, how the turmoil of her childhood had made her cling to routines, long for safety and security.

Did he have a right to do this? To ask this of her? It was too late for doubts. He had done it. He was aware he was holding his breath.

"Yes," she whispered.

And Valentino began to breathe again.

Erin could not believe what was happening to her life. Was this how you were rewarded for toasting the universe with *to surprises*?

She, Erin O'Rourke, Canadian account clerk whose only claim to fame was her father's skiing career, was on a private jet.

A royal jet.

The aircraft, staffed with uniformed people, had more opulent furnishings than most houses she had been in. It was more luxurious than the presidential suite that Valentino had inhabited at the Northern Lights Hotel.

There was even a bedroom, a master suite she had glimpsed on their way to the main cabin area. It was a beautiful space of many cushions, gray silks and deep walnuts. It made her heart hammer to think of doing some of the things they had done up here at thirty thousand feet. She was stunned by how the exoticness of that possibility stirred something in her that she had not known she possessed.

However, on their last night in the cabin in her world—the one that had become their world—Valentino had briefed her a bit on protocol.

How to address his mother when they met. How to handle salutes, attention, the press. Reluctantly, he had informed her, there was one area of their life they would have to put on hold as they entered his world.

Even if he had not told her, she would have known as soon as they got on the jet. She would have known by the way he avoided taking her hand, touching her, that they had entered a place where he had to be extraordinarily careful. Where they would both have to be extraordinarily careful if they did not want to earn the censure of the palace and the clamoring of the press.

It might have all been a little overwhelming except for the fact Harvey was in a basket in her lap, letting her know he was mightily unimpressed with his first trip in an airplane and overseas. He yawned and licked a paw.

And, of course, Valentino was at her side.

It was slightly unsettling to see he was addressed, always, as Your Highness, or sir. It was slightly unsettling to think all of this was his.

His hand found hers and gave it a quick squeeze before letting it go again as they prepared for takeoff. She realized, when he let go, that the unabashed passion they had for each other at the cabin would not be appropriate here.

Obviously, because of his position, the very physical part of their relationship needed to be reined in for appearances' sake.

For some reason, that made her nearly breathless with wanting him. Erin took his hand, surreptitiously ran her thumb over his wrist, until he looked at her with such heat, she thought she would melt.

A staff member came to speak to them. She slid her hand from his and looked out the window, smiling.

For all that he was a prince, Valentino was still the one who had given her a sense of discovering the new in her own world.

The one who was leading her now into this brand-new world. This was no time to be afraid. It was time to accept that life was an incredible adventure.

She had accepted the invitation.

She had to throw herself into it. There was no room here for that girl who harbored, always, the sense of not being good enough.

Indeed, it felt as if Valentino's attention to her had erased that part of her forever.

As soon as Erin stepped out the door of the plane, she knew she was in a magical place. The sun was warm but gentle on her face, like a kiss. The air held the mingled perfumes of spice and flowers.

From that first step, she entered the most extraordinary experience of her life determined to embrace every single thing about it.

A royal limousine met them and whisked them down narrow streets with whitewashed medieval buildings that seemed to lean over the streets, keeping the sun from reaching the cobblestones. Flowers cascaded out of the high window boxes that the sun touched. In places, colorful clotheslines, two stories up, spanned the street. Though the car was air-conditioned, Erin opened the windows to fully experience not just the sights but the sounds and smells of Valentino's home.

She could hear strains of music pouring out windows, laughter, a lovers' squabble, children shrieking, dogs barking. The air was redolent with scent: spicy cooking smells, exotic flowers, the sun on the white bricks.

It was fantastic.

The palace sat at the edge of those crooked streets, jumbled buildings, houses stacked up hillsides.

The cheerful chaos was left behind them as imposing wrought-iron gates swung open to lush expanses of lawn, gorgeous gardens, gurgling fountains. And at the end of a long, curving driveway, a palace.

It was not the typical "fairy-tale" palace, like Neuschwanstein Castle in Germany, but rather an imposing and majestic square. Constructed of huge white-marble blocks, the severity of the structure was diluted by the exquisitely carved detail around the doors and windows, the intricate designs on the caps that topped pillars, the lush vines that crawled up the walls, and the huge concrete vats of flowers that abounded.

Once inside the palace, Erin could not keep her mouth from popping open in astonishment. Though it was warm outside, the inside of the building was cool. As Valentino took her through to her suite, there was almost too much to take in: gorgeous gilt-framed paintings, chandeliers that dripped priceless crystals, hand-carved wainscoting, silk wallpapers, detailed tapestries and hand-knotted rugs.

Her suite was as ornate as the rest of the palace. She looked around, terrified to touch anything. It was his touch that grounded her.

By themselves, finally, he gathered her to him, covered her in kisses. Her ears, her eyelids, her neck, finally her lips.

"I've been longing to do that all day," he said huskily in her ear.

"Me, too," she said, taking his hand and pulling him toward the bedroom. "Should we—"

He backed away from her. "Sorceress," he said. "Sadly, there are no secrets in the palace. Your stay here will be a chaste one."

She looked at his lips and felt longing rip through her. Seeing him in this world—and their relationship being forbidden fruit—made her want to be exactly what he had called her. A sorceress, tempting him. She took a step toward him, but he laughed, shook his head and slipped out the door.

She found her way to her bedroom—a huge, carved four-poster was at the center of it. Tapestries hung on the walls.

Who does the dusting? She wondered practically.

There was a lovely pillowed bed for Harvey. The thought of a litterbox in this space made her wince, but still there was one, placed subtly in a closet.

She put Harvey on the bed. He sniffed it and settled himself approvingly on what she was fairly certain was pure silk.

Her suitcase had arrived before her—it had not touched her hands once since she had packed it—and now it had been unpacked for her! It made her wish she'd had time to invest in new underwear! She hadn't been prepared for the fact people would be touching her things.

She went through to the adjoining bathroom. The tub, veined marble, was large enough to swim in. The fixtures were gold—and probably the real thing.

She suddenly felt overwhelmed. The plane, and now this. Plus, unspoken rules around being with the man she had become so comfortable with. She felt she was being plunged into a world where she could never belong.

And yet when Valentino came to collect her, her doubts were erased, again, by the look in his eyes. He stepped inside her room, took her face in both hands, and kissed her deeply and passionately.

"Don't do that and expect a chaste relationship," she warned him.

"You're right. It won't do to have you glow-ing with passion at the moment. Should we get meeting my mother over with?"

"Is it going to be horrible?" she asked.

"Of course," he said with a grin.

But it wasn't horrible. His mother was at a table in an ornate sitting room, which was a relief, since Erin thought she might be sitting on a throne with a crown on her head.

Instead, she was having tea, with a dog at her feet. She was also wearing a dress that might be called dowdy, if one dared to call the queen's dress dowdy, even in their own mind.

It was obvious where Valentino had gotten his good looks from.

They sat at the table with her, and a servant poured tea. Valentino introduced Erin as his friend. His mother, the queen, had obviously been putting people at ease her entire life and she was very, very gracious.

"I understand you love animals," she said, and Erin realized she had been *briefed*—given one detail about her—to make her feel welcomed. The queen was also good at not showing what she really felt. Though she was extremely charming, there was an impenetrable quality to her charm and her eyes were guarded.

They mostly discussed Harvey and the dog who snoozed at her feet.

"See?" Valentino teased her as they left the audience, "You survived."

"I feel kind of sorry for her," Erin admitted.

"For my mother?" he asked, incredulous.

"I get a sense of no one knowing her. Of deep loneliness. I—I'm sorry. I shouldn't have said that." There was probably a law against making observations about the queen!

But Valentino was looking at her, a small smile playing across his lips.

"You see, Erin? You see what others do not. They see her wealth, her power, her privilege, her station. Everyone wants something from her. It makes it impossible to trust, to be liked for herself alone. You see the heart she has never felt safe to show anyone."

His voice dropped. "It is the life you are saving me from."

After the audience with the queen, they seemed to be free, but with parameters. They had dinner that night in a small walled garden off her suite. Even though an exquisite meal had been left for them, and they were not interrupted, Erin was aware they were not really alone.

"Are there people everywhere?" she whispered to him. "Hovering in the shadows, waiting for you to need something?"

"I'm afraid so."

And so even after the delicious food, it felt as if they were starving. To touch each other. It was strangely tantalizing, their relationship suddenly fraught with suspense. Anticipation.

They got up from the table and Valentino led her to the darkest corner of the garden. He claimed, loudly, he wanted to show her a white flower that looked particularly stunning at night.

Instead, he pressed her up against the garden wall and ravaged her mouth, kissing her until they were both frantic with need.

Valentino yanked away from her when they heard the clink of dishware being cleared from the table in the garden. Erin giggled breathlessly. He ran a frustrated hand through the dark tangle of his curls.

"I thought my family left torture behind in the Dark Ages," he muttered.

The dishes clattered more loudly. They waited until the sounds stopped and then, like errant teenagers—and with all the same pent-up longing—went to their separate quarters.

As he showed her his country, they traveled in a three-car entourage. The first day they brought Harvey, but after that, to her shock, the cat agreed to tolerate Milo as his babysitter. She exchanged phone numbers, making Milo promise to call if there were any problems. She reminded herself—a little pathetically—of a nervous mother.

She had rarely been without the cat for over a year since his eyesight and hearing had started failing so badly, but she knew she was being silly. Milo had her phone number. She had his.

Valentino was an incredible tour guide, well versed in his country's colorful history, proud of its many accomplishments, passionate about the roads forward into the future. The country was amazing, but it was also amazing to see Valentino in this element. His element.

In the cabin, he had been exploring a new world. Eager, to be sure, but adorably inept at so many practical things.

Now, she saw the man that he truly was: confident, polished, comfortable with his position and power.

It heightened her already over-the-top awareness of him and a new tension sizzled between them. His hand reaching for hers nearly scorched her. Stolen kisses had the intensity of exploding rockets. His gaze resting on her could make her heart start beating so hard it felt as if it would break out of her chest.

After they had toured the ruins of one castle, they came out to find the road on both sides lined with people.

"Word must have got out that I was here," he said. "You don't mind if we stop, do you?"

"Of course not." Uncertainty hit her. "Do you want me to wait in the car?"

"No!"

She could tell his security team, who traveled in cars in front and behind them, especially Colonel Del Rento, hated this spontaneous stop as much as he loved it. It was evident he was admired and adored by the people of his country, and that he reciprocated those feelings.

He introduced her to the people as his friend. In some ways, it was not completely unfamiliar. At the height of her father's career, this is what it had been like traveling with him. People had recognized him, wanted his autograph, wanted to speak to him. Sometimes, quite a crush of people would form around him.

The big difference was that with her father, he had enjoyed the attention immensely because it had been all about *him*.

Erin noticed Valentino's utter and sincere interest in people. He smiled, clapped a shoulder, threw back his head and laughed. He would bend close to hear more clearly.

As with her father, when she sometimes had received reflected attention, mostly of the *Are you going to be a ski star, too?* variety, some people were very aware of her. Embarrassingly, one older lady curtsied. A little girl presented her with a hastily gathered bouquet of crushed flowers.

Her nose buried in those lovely flowers, Erin noticed Valentino being passed a baby boy. Something in her went very still as Valentino handled the baby with an ease that was unusual in a single man. He admired him and kissed his fat cheek before handing him back.

He, Erin thought, before she could stop herself, *is going to make a great father.*

The thought discombobulated her. He had made it clear, when he had come to the cabin, when he had brought her here, that he wanted to see what the future held for him.

He had introduced her to his mother.

Now, he was introducing her to his people.

Her future could be him. This land. His babies. A euphoria swept through her. It was quite unlike anything she had ever felt before.

It only grew as she watched him talk to one of the people in his entourage when they got back to the cars. Quietly, he was giving names and instructions: make sure we find out about crop insurance; send flowers to that woman, she's lost her husband; make sure that baby gets a teddy bear.

What she didn't like about traveling with him was the sense of constant surveillance—though it made those kisses stolen in that tiny cave at the base of the ruin even more sizzling—and the fact they were not free to be spontaneous. Erin longed to immerse herself in the noisy marketplaces, to have coffee and pastry at one of those outdoor cafés. But that was not his life.

Her favorite thing became the visit to the beach at the end of each day of sightseeing. While the front of the palace faced sweeping lawns and gardens, the back of it was perched on a rocky outcrop that overlooked the sea.

To Erin's delight, Valentino showed her a secret set of stairs cut into the granite that led to a gorgeous, private, white-sand beach.

Here, finally—save for Harvey, who had yowled his dismay when she had tried to leave him yet again—they were alone. They were children again—as playful on that beach as they had been at her cabin. They built sand-castles. They played in the turquoise waters, running, splashing each other. There were snorkels, and Valentino showed her the magical world that existed right below the surface of the sea. They stole kisses and touched sun-warmed skin.

Today, after a long day of sightseeing, Erin lay on a blanket. She was wearing a bikini that a few weeks ago she would not have worn. But a new her—a bolder her—was confident in herself and her body, that confidence born of the fire in Valentino's eyes when he saw her in bathing suits. She found she quite enjoyed tormenting him, pushing him to break out of the chaste prison his position put them both in.

The waves came up and he grabbed a surf-board.

"I'll show you how," he said.

For all the age-old beauty of his country, for all that she loved every minute together, how could she not love these moments best of all? Alone. Playing. Touching each other.

Standing on the surfboard was a lot harder than it looked. Soon, they were both soaked, gulping down water as they gurgled with laughter. Erin had finally just managed to stand when she saw a little gray head, bobbing toward her. Harvey had fallen in the water!

"Valentino! Save him!"

Valentino hurled himself through the water,

but as she watched the rescue, she realized her crazy cat was paddling around, perfectly content.

She was laughing so hard, she had to hoist herself up on the surfboard. "Have you ever seen anything like that before?"

His laughter joined hers, and he made it to the cat. He scooped Harvey, soaked, out of the water, came back and placed him in front of her on the surfboard she had straddled.

"Tigers swim," he told the cat. "You wonderful old warrior. You are part tiger, aren't you?"

Harvey preened.

And then Valentino put his hand on the back of Erin's neck and tugged her mouth to his. The kiss tasted of the sea. And of sand. Of the sun's warmth. Of things new. And of things ancient. The kiss tasted of promises.

It had a texture of its own: Erin could feel her future painting itself as his mouth claimed hers. The euphoria intensified until it was like a physical tingling inside her skin trying to get out.

They had been building to this moment for days, the anticipation of it razor-sharp between them. Now it was here, every physical longing, like too much water in a dam, suddenly bursting free.

She was hungry for him. Starving. And he was hungry for her. His mouth ravaged her willing mouth. He kissed the sun-warmed tops of her breasts, owning her, claiming her, letting his lips tell her *I need you. I can't live without you.*

It felt as if she could not live one more moment without the beautiful intimacy between them. She drew his head from her breast, claimed his lips, tasted him.

And then a drone came overhead and swooped down toward them, buzzing like a bothersome fly. She lost her balance and the surfboard tilted, sending her and Harvey into the water. She surfaced, sputtering and gasping.

Valentino rescued them both, one arm holding the cat, the other protectively around her shoulder as he got them back to the sand.

As he broke away from her, he sent a fearsome glare to the drone and then gave her a look, impotent and furious, at the pleasure denied them once again.

CHAPTER FOURTEEN

VALENTINO AWOKE AND was aware of an ache of need within him. His first thought was of Erin and how his need to touch her, to kiss her, to have her, had been thwarted.

That drone, yesterday afternoon. He sighed. The reality of the world. His world.

Mostly, though, he loved showing her that world.

Loved her wonder, her enthusiasm, her delight. He was experiencing his realm through her and it seemed as brand-new and as shiny as a bright copper penny.

But he missed waking to her in the morning, as if he had done it his whole life, not just for a few days in a cabin in the middle of nowhere.

It occurred to him he was edging closer.

Not edging, really. Barreling. He had seen the look in her eyes when he had held that baby. He wanted to spend the rest of his life with her. He wanted her to have his children. He wanted her to be his queen.

There was a soft rap at the door.

Milo came in bearing a tray with coffee and a selection of local morning papers. Valentino would take breakfast in the garden, later, with Erin. He was aware that he was eager to see her, as if the gold of her hair and the green of her eyes were as new to him as that bright penny.

Today, they would go to see the olive groves in the south. He hoped to get her on a horse. She had never ridden before, and there was no better way to see the groves. He couldn't wait to share this activity that he loved with her. He hoped she would take to it, that someday she would ride as wonderfully as she skied...

Finally, he came out of his thoughts and noticed Milo was still standing there, a funny look on his face.

"Is something the matter?"

"Sir, the papers—" Milo looked so distressed.

Valentino picked up the first paper.

He looked at the front-page picture. It was of him and Erin in the water, just after they had kissed. Even though they had missed him lowering his head to her breast, it was a shamelessly intrusive photo.

The press—still hoping to milk a little more from both his and Angelica's lives—tried to follow them every time they stepped out of the palace. Thankfully, the staff had become masters at distraction, sending them in the wrong direction, dispatching decoy cars so that Erin and Valentino weren't always on display. No drones were allowed in the air within a mile of his entourage.

But yesterday that one had slipped in from the other side of the island, coming over that cliff before he'd been able to protect Erin from it.

Valentino frowned as he saw that something had been circled in the picture, and that an arrow showed an inset picture with a blow-up of the circled item.

It was Harvey, soaked, looking like a drowned rat, sitting between Erin's legs on the surfboard.

In his language, the headline blared *Crazy Cat Lady!*

There were several papers here, and he looked through them all. Each one had the same photo—sold, no doubt, to the highest bidders—and a variation of the crazy cat lady story.

It filled him with fury like nothing he had ever felt. How dare they miss her incredible beauty, her wonder at life, and expose something so banal? How dare they zero in on this minute detail about her, and blow it up cruelly and with such exclusive focus? Why wouldn't they see her love of an aging cat for what it was? Tender? Compassionate? *Good*.

His rage intensified when he realized he was powerless against it.

He looked at Milo. They had come a long, long way since that day when Milo had gleefully announced to Erin that Valentino was going to marry someone else.

Valentino was fairly certain that Milo was nearly as enchanted with Erin as he himself was. He adored the cat!

Milo gave him a look of pure sympathy, understanding the prince's position, maybe before he, himself, fully got it.

Valentino loved her.

He loved Erin O'Rourke madly and beyond reason. He would do anything for her. He would die to protect her.

He was suddenly and sharply aware of the demands of holding a position in a royal household. Could he invite Erin, someone he cared about deeply—that he loved deeply—into the kind of life where the public pressures could be so cruel and unrelenting? Angelica had rejected it, and she had been born to it.

How unfair would it be to ask someone who didn't know the full weight of it to share this life with him?

Share this life with him?

He had become too caught up in it all. The passion had swept away his ability to be rational. The joy he had felt in her presence had made him, selfishly, just want more and more and more.

Of laughter. Of conversation. Of *wanting* with an unholy need.

How could he even consider the possibility of her and him together—forever—when he would never be able to protect her from *this*? From her life being put under a microscope; for her eccentricities to be exposed to a mean-spirited world.

She had told him about withdrawing from ski racing because she was so sensitive to her father's criticism, the expectations placed on her by the press.

How much worse would this be? A collective critical spirit aimed right at her. The person she was—who had grown up in the sanctuary of those beautiful mountains—could be destroyed by this relentless attention, this cutting meanness, this desire to focus on fault.

It was a repeating story within royal families. The outsider was brought in. Some fool thought love would be enough. And it never, ever, was.

It had already started. With the cat. Then it would be her hair, or a dress she chose, or an extra pound put on, or a gaffe at a royal function. They would tear away at her like vultures on carrion, making her smaller and smaller...

He could not stand the pain of what he was seeing as her possible future if he brought her into his world. He threw down the paper and gave Milo a look.

"How can you love someone and do this to them?" Valentino asked, his voice hoarse with pain. "Ask this of them?"

He supposed he hoped Milo would have an answer, would hold out hope, would help him see things from a different perspective.

Instead, the man looked absolutely crushed—as if he had just seen a place of complete light turn dark—as he turned and left the room.

Erin looked at the note from Valentino. He had canceled their plans for today. She had been so looking forward to the olive groves. He had been going to show her how to ride. The thought was terrifying. And exciting. That was exactly what her feelings were of late: terrified and excited.

Every single thing they did together shone with a light.

He said he would be busy today, that something unexpected had come up, but if she would join him for dinner in the garden, he would be honored.

She had a lovely day. Despite being shadowed by security, she finally was able to go to a market. She had a rich and chocolatey cup of coffee and a sumptuous pastry at a local café. No one paid the least attention to her.

She felt as if she was absorbing Valentino's country through her pores. What she noticed was the softness of it, in stark contrast to her own home of harsh climates and landscapes.

Here, everything was soft: the light, the heat, the rolling landscapes, the flavors. She was falling in love with Valentino's beautiful island nation every bit as much as she was falling in love with him.

That truth warmed her, as rich and delightful as the drink she was sipping.

She loved him. Loved him. Loved him. Loved him.

The phrase was still repeating in her mind on an endless delicious loop as she entered the garden just as dusk was falling. The perfume of flowers was heavy in the air. A table had been set on the lawn. It was romantic, with a beautiful linen tablecloth, flickering candles, places already set. The stars winked like diamonds in the black-velvet sky above the garden.

Obviously, Valentino had planned a romantic dinner for two.

Her heart stopped as she saw him pacing back and forth near the back wall. He seemed nervous, and it was so unlike him. Her eyes went from him to the beautiful table setting.

He was going to propose.

He saw her and stopped. For a moment, she saw something in his face that terrified her—a sadness so acute, she wondered if someone had died.

"No Harvey tonight?" he said as he came and greeted her with the traditional kiss on each cheek.

"Milo is quite taken with him. The feeling seems to be mutual."

He glanced toward the sky. "Let's hope for some privacy," he said. "If a drone comes, we'll move inside."

The thought of the drone seemed to upset him, added to an almost agitated air about him. Something she was not accustomed to.

They sat and he poured wine. He drank his too fast, in two gigantic gulps. A feast had been put before them. It sometimes seemed as if the kitchen staff were trying to outdo

themselves in their efforts to show her the
wonders of their island cuisine. It was so endearing. She had made a point of going to
the kitchen after every meal and discussing
it with them. Thanking the chef.

Why was Valentino so not himself? Was
he going to propose? Somehow, she would
not have imagined it like this.

Had she imagined it? Him proposing?

Of course she had! She had imagined him
on one knee, his eyes—those oh-so-familiar
deep brown eyes—resting on her face, filled
with tenderness and hope.

Will you...?

Yet tonight his expression was anything
but tender.

Finally, she could not get on with the pre-
tense of enjoying dinner any longer. She set
down her fork.

"What is wrong?" she asked.

He hesitated. He looked anywhere but at
her. But then he did look at her, drew in a
deep breath, set his shoulders.

"We've made a mistake."

Her mouth fell open. This was so far from
what she'd expected.

"I'm sorry," she stammered. "What?"

"Not we. Me. I'm sorry. It's unfolded too
quickly."

She stared at him, not believing what she was hearing. This was the same man who had trailed his fingers across the heated surface of her skin. Insatiable. Who had stood on top of an igloo with her. Who had swam, laughing in the sea with her just yesterday, splashing her, chasing her around through the waves. Who had stolen kisses as if he could not get enough of her.

The man who had held that baby and filled her with the most terrifying thing of all...hope.

"I don't understand," she said. His face was so remote, the Valentino she thought she knew replaced with the suave and distant stranger.

She said she didn't understand. But she was beginning to, she just didn't want to.

Her life was playing out in a constant, nauseating loop: she expected one thing and the exact opposite happened.

Twice now, she had expected a proposal and gotten this instead.

Why was she so surprised? Had she really thought she was a girl who could hold a man like Valentino's interest?

Even Paul, the most ordinary of guys, had seen her for what she was.

Beyond ordinary.

Boring.

Valentino wouldn't even look at her. He looked at his hand. He was grasping the stem of his wineglass so tight, it looked as if he might snap it.

He said, "Erin, there's someone else."

She heard shame in his voice. And defeat.

Love turned to hate in the blink of an eye. The euphoria that she had been floating on since she had arrived at Valentino's home hissed out of her, air out of a pricked balloon. She could feel everything inside her collapsing—as if a bomb had been dropped—into the space that had been filled with wonder, with discovery, with bravery, with a sense of adventure.

How could he do this to her?

How could he bring her all the way here to cut the legs out from under her like this?

The awful truth hit her. She had never known him. Not at all. She had believed what she'd wanted to believe, built a fairy tale around him.

The only part of the fairy tale that was true was that he was a prince.

She should have obeyed her instincts. They had warned her he was an ass. She would not give him the satisfaction of spitting those furious words at him, of letting him know how deeply she was wounded.

She got up carefully from the table. With

her spine ramrod-straight, she walked away from him. She did not look back.

Valentino watched her go. Shored up by some innate dignity, by a strength she might not have even been aware she possessed, it struck him that Erin O'Rourke moved like a queen.

He turned away from the sight, from her absolute bravery in the face of his betrayal. He was afraid if he watched any longer, he would scream *No, I didn't mean it. It was all lies. Come back.*

He shouldn't have said the last part. The most awful lie of all, about there being some-one else.

But he needed Erin not just to go but to never look back. He needed what had flashed through her eyes for him: pure and primal disgust. Maybe even hatred.

He needed those things because, if she looked back, he was not sure he would be strong enough to do what he had to do.

He needed to save her. And that meant let-ting her go.

If he loved her, truly, he needed to send her back to her old life before it was too late, before she was so notorious that—because of him—there could never be an old life to go back to.

CHAPTER FIFTEEN

ERIN WAS NOT even sure how she and Harvey got home. The journey was a blur. Somehow she had been back on that jet. Valentino must have arranged that in his eagerness to erase his *mistake,* to get rid of her.

For days after arriving at the resort, she felt as if she was in a fog. She could not bring herself to go to the cabin, to see if anything remained of their igloo and angels.

She went over the day before his horrible announcement with a fine-tooth comb. What had she said? What had she done that was so wrong? Why had he pulled the plug so suddenly? How could there be someone else when they had spent every waking moment together?

It must be someone from his past. Someone who had come forward after they had heard about his split from Angelica. It had to be someone more suited than her.

Erin also tried to figure out how she could be feeling one thing—she loved him, loved him, loved him—and he quite another. How was that possible without her awareness? And yet it was an awful, awful repeat of what had happened with Paul.

During the day, she was able to turn her mind to work, to other things, but in her dreams, she was with him, laughing. She would awake to a sense of grief.

Still, Erin surprised herself, too. She did not retreat from life. She did not hide out in her apartment going over things endlessly.

She found an almost shocking core of strength.

Each day Erin felt a little more certainty, a quiet confidence, that that she had never felt before. Increasingly, she was aware she might not be sure who Valentino really was, and in fact, it was quite likely she was never going to unravel the mystery of him.

But she was sure who she was.

Ironically, it was the time she had spent with him that had awakened this new confidence in her, a quiet sense of herself.

She became aware that her insecurities were rooted in her father's criticisms. She had developed a sense of not being good enough.

When he and her mother had split, she had

taken on bits of that, too. What could she have done to save her family? If she had been a different person, a better person—if she had kept skiing competitively—would it all have turned out differently?

That is why she had accepted Paul, forgiving his slights, his insults, his lack of enthusiasm for her and their relationship. Because she had felt that was all she deserved. She had accepted what she thought she could get.

Despite the bad ending with Valentino, she had *grown* in the context of loving him. She had become *more* than she was before.

Even Kelly noticed the changes in her. "You're different," she said.

Erin didn't even have to ask her how. She could *feel* some basic difference in herself, born of shared laughter, of quiet talks, of heated looks and touches. Born of being with a person where she had become more completely herself than she had ever been before: silly, strong, adventurous, bold, shy.

And despite her new strength, she indulged one weakness. Erin scoured the tabloids, online and paper copies, looking for some news of him, a glimpse of him, a look at his new lover.

But each day passed with nothing.

How was that possible? He had done everything in his power to try to keep their budding relationship away from prying eyes and he had not been successful.

In fact, just this morning, there had been a text. It was the first she had heard from anyone from her days with the prince. Milo had her phone number because he had cared for the cat.

She'd been terrified—and hopeful—when his name popped up.

Terrified that he was sending bad news about Valentino. Or a picture of the new love that she told herself she could handle seeing.

When she looked at the photo—no text, no message—she was not sure why he had sent it.

It was a photograph of the front of a newspaper, from when she'd been there. That day that Harvey had swam with them. She vaguely remembered a drone coming over.

She wasn't able to read the headline—it was in their language. But looking at that picture, at both of them laughing, of Harvey perched on the surfboard, Erin felt exactly as she did when she first woke up every morning.

Grief-stricken.

She had closed the picture right away, feeling it robbing her hard-earned strength, feeling angry at Milo for sending it.

Partway through the day, it nagged at her. Why had Milo sent the newspaper article? It wasn't as if she could understand it.

Still, on her lunch hour, she felt compelled to open it again. She stared at the picture. Such love! How could it—

She looked at the headline. Surely, in this day and age, she could translate what it said? Sure enough, she found an app on her phone and carefully typed in the exact lettering.

That didn't seem right.

The translation must be wrong.

Crazy Cat Lady!

Erin went very still. She got it. She got it completely.

The papers were making fun of her.

Valentino didn't have a new love interest.

He was doing what he perceived he needed to do to protect her. Just as with Angelica, he was willing to be the one who took it, who paid the price, who made the sacrifice.

For her.

To keep her safe.

She thought of his mother and the wariness in her; the loneliness she had seen in the cool shadows of the queen's eyes.

That was what Valentino was sentencing

himself to. That was what he was prepared to do *for her*. That is what he thought love was.

And that was what he thought of her. That she wasn't strong enough. That he had to take it for her.

She saw Milo's sending the picture for exactly what it was.

A challenge to be more than she had ever been before: braver, stronger, more certain.

She saw it for its purpose.

To intervene like this, Milo must be extraordinarily worried about Valentino.

Erin knew what she had to do. She had to gamble that she was right. She had to trust that what had unfolded between them was real.

The most real thing that she had ever experienced.

She had to act more fearlessly than she ever had before.

Valentino was putting himself in a lonely prison because he thought she needed rescuing.

Oh, the irony. It was not her who needed rescuing! It was him.

She had to rescue the prince.

"Sir, there's someone here to see you."

"I'm not receiving today." Valentino saw

the distress on Milo's face. It had been growing for days.

Valentino, on those odd days when he glanced at himself in the mirror, could see why. He looked awful. He was losing weight alarmingly. He was unshaven. There were dark circles under his eyes. His dreams were the dreams of a man tormented by what he had lost.

He knew he had done what he'd had to do.

But he had not expected to be haunted so completely by the look on Erin's face when he had betrayed her.

Surely, he could have done it differently? Surely, he could have made her see reason without hurting her so badly?

Milo left the room, shutting the door quietly behind him, and Valentino wandered over to his window. His beautiful land had been stripped of its color. He was blind to beauty now.

He should have just told her he was dying. It felt more true than what he had said.

He heard the door whisper open.

"Milo! Leave me! I don't want anything." Especially not him hovering with *that* look on his face.

Milo didn't answer and he turned to glare at him.

His world stopped. As he drank her in—the shining waterfall of her hair, the green of her eyes, the pale rose of her lips—he was aware of seeing color for the first time in weeks.

He could feel the weakness in him, as if he were a man drowning and a life ring was within reach. But what if you had to sacrifice someone else to save your own life?

He did not think he had any strength left. Not one ounce.

Yet he found just enough to lift an eyebrow at her, to strip the sigh within him from his voice. "How did you get here?"

"I flew. I had to bring my broom since I didn't have the private jet at my disposal."

Her words transported him back to the very beginning when he had teased her about her fairy-tale cottage minus the child-eating witch.

This was not the time for jokes. Though, when she said it, her voice so light, like music, he could feel himself leaning toward her, leaning toward the memory of their shared laughter, leaning toward a quiet strength in her eyes.

How was it she looked so much better than she ever had, when he was so much worse?

Really, just confirmation he had done the right thing.

"I had to leave Harvey," she said. "I couldn't figure out the intricacies of traveling with him. Kelly is looking after him."

"You left Harvey?" A strange panic welled up in him. She'd only leave Harvey if it was an emergency. What if she had come to give him some awful news?

"I know. Your tabloids will be disappointed when they find out. Crazy Cat Lady with no cat."

"That was cruel of them," he said. "I'm sorry you had to see it."

She looked at him gravely then came and touched his arm. Her touch on his arm made him close his eyes and just drink in the way her closeness felt.

When he finally opened his eyes again, she was looking at him with an unsettling *knowing*. *A*s if the gig was up. As if she knew everything.

"It's okay," she said soothingly. "I'm okay."

He heard the truth in that. And wondered again at the unfairness of it. How could she be okay when he was not?

"This time," he growled at her. "What about next time? What about when they are tearing into you about your clothes, or your accent, or the fact you used the wrong fork at a state dinner? What then?"

She didn't seem to get the seriousness of this at all. She was smiling at him, ever so tenderly.

"Is that why you lied to me?" she asked.

He stiffened. "What makes you think I lied?"

"To protect me."

He made one last effort. He gathered all his strength. He said, "No! There is some-one else."

"Uh-huh," she said with aggravating and patent disbelief.

"Don't you know who I am?" he said. "People believe me."

"Maybe people who don't know you."

Every moment they had ever spent together seemed to flash before his eyes. It was true. She knew him like no one else ever had. Or ever would again.

"Valentino," she said firmly, "there is no one else."

"How do you know?" he demanded with what was left of his strength.

She cocked her head at him. "Okay. Tell me the color of her hair."

But he could not think of any hair color except the sun-on-wheat color right in front of him.

"Eyes?" she prodded him.

Green. It was the only color he could think of.

"What do you feel like when she kisses you?"

His eyes fastened on her lips and the memories seared through him white-hot.

"That's what I thought," she said. "There is no one else. I know. I know by looking at you. I should have known right away that it was a lie."

What could he say? He couldn't very well produce evidence it wasn't a lie.

"I had to make you go," he whispered.

"Because of the story," she concluded. "You thought I would be hurt by the story, by being called names."

"It wasn't just that story. It was all the stories that would come. It would be watching, helpless, as they pecked away at you. It was what a life with me would steal from you."

"You understand what you're saying, don't you?"

"Completely," he said.

"That you love me. You love me so much, you would sacrifice your own chance at happiness to protect me."

He was silent. She was so smart. Why had he thought he could fool her for any length of time?

"The irony is, Valentino, that to be the

woman worthy of that love, I have to be willing to risk the arrows. I have to be strong. I can't let you protect me. I can't let you sacrifice yourself for what you perceive as my well-being.

"I don't think a life with you could steal anything of value from me. It would just give and give and give.

"Love and love and more love.

"And I'm not leaving you. No matter what you say or do, I can see your truth in your face. I can see it in how you've suffered—look at you—to protect me.

"Here's where you have it all wrong—you are not a prince riding in to rescue me. You will always be to me, first and foremost, a man not a prince.

"You will always be, to me, the one I would risk everything to rescue."

Her words poured over him like a warm balm over a raw wound. "You're turning the fairy tales on their head," he finally said.

She smiled at him. "I know, Valentino. I know."

And he could resist no longer. He reached for the life ring she had thrown him. He allowed himself to be rescued by her love. He went into her arms and laid his head on her shoulder, the warrior home from the war.

"Erin," he whispered, his voice hoarse and raw, the warrior's surrender complete, "I love you. I will love you forever."

Valentino watched Erin come across the meadow toward him. Summer had come to the mountains and the clearing, once filled with snow angels, was now filled with wildflowers. She wore a ring of them in the hair, which flowed freely onto her shoulders, bare to the sun.

She was wearing a white dress, though he was not sure he would have called it a bridal gown. She carried a basket, Harvey lolling in it contentedly, as if he, not she, was the star of today's show.

Valentino wondered: did all grooms feel this way as their bride came toward them? On top of the world? Like the luckiest man alive? Anointed by a mysterious force? Made strong and whole, not by their own power, but by love?

Erin could have had the wedding of the century. She could have worn a gown encrusted with jewels and a priceless lace veil that had been passed down for centuries. She could have had her wedding in a cathedral with a full children's choir, with a carriage waiting outside the door to carry them through the streets of the country that had come to adore her during the short days of their courtship.

Indeed, that wedding Erin had rejected, was what his mother had wanted. And her father, Enrique, would have been beside himself with delight if the wedding had been conducted with pomp and circumstance.

But this was Erin's day and she knew exactly what she wanted.

In the last few months, she had come into herself in ways that were as unexpected as they were wonderful. She *shone* with life. She had a unique ability to embrace the unexpected. The love flowed out of her and embraced everyone that she touched, which was why she had become so beloved to his people in such a short time.

But she had held firm about today.

She wanted to celebrate, not who they were publicly but what this cottage and this meadow had given them.

Whenever they were here, they were just two people and it was love that crowned them, love that lent them its glory.

In light of how difficult it was to keep a secret, to keep things private, it was something of a miracle that they had managed to have only a few other people here: Milo, Kelly, Ricky and an officiant.

In a short while, a helicopter would whisk the visitors away.

And they would be home.

Not in this meadow, as much as they loved it, and not in the cottage.

Home was where they were, together.

Forever.

EPILOGUE

THIS, VALENTINO THOUGHT, was possibly one of the hardest things he had ever done. He held the cat in his arms, wrapped in a hand-made blanket that had been a gift to Harvey from Milo.

Milo, who never stopped—even though more than a year had passed—trying to make it up to his princess, to Erin, that he had been the one who had delivered the cruel news of Valentino's engagement to Angelica.

Erin was at Valentino's side, the baby due any day, tears streaming down her face, as they made their way to the small walled garden where they still made time for each other every single day and shared romantic meals.

Even now it occurred to him how Harvey had protected Erin right until the end. Except for his increasing blindness and inability to hear, there had been no long illness, no injuries, no loss of appetite or interest in life.

They had just woken up this morning and Harvey had looked for all the world as if he was asleep in his basket next to their bed. In fact, they had gone out and had breakfast before noticing he had not joined them, as he usually would at the first sniff of food.

The cat had not been asleep.

Valentino had notified the gardener, who had dug a small hole and now waited beside it, head bowed, shovel in hand.

The gardener must have told others because staff were now streaming into the garden, silent and respectful as Valentino knelt and laid Harvey in the tiny grave.

Valentino touched the blanket and said out loud, "Your work here is done, old warrior. You truly had the heart of a tiger. But it's my job now. You rest in peace, knowing I will make her feel safe. Cherished. Listened to."

If it was hard for Erin, in her condition, to get down, it didn't seem like it. She knelt by the grave, touched her fingers to her lips and then to that blanket.

"Thank you," she whispered. "My friend."

In her new language she whispered, *"Beloved."*

Valentino drew her to her feet and put his arm around her shoulders. She turned her face into him and cried as the gardener silently shoveled.

When he was done, Valentino lifted her chin and nodded over his shoulder to direct her attention to what was happening.

They were coming forward, the palace staff, one by one. Each of them held a single flower, which they laid on that small heap of rich, newly turned black soil until it was blanketed with bright blossoms.

Harvey had become quite famous. Rather than shirking the *Crazy Cat Lady* title the press had so maliciously branded her with in those first public days of their relationship, Erin had embraced it. Soon, Harvey had his own social media accounts and his own channel on the streaming service. At first, it was only the people of Canada and Lorenzo del Toro who embraced Harvey.

But then he had become a media sensation with millions of followers and millions of views of his videos, which were sometimes nothing more than him snoring softly on top of Milo's blanket in his basket. In the fall, they had allowed a charity to make a calendar of him and the sales had been through the roof.

The cat, according to experts in such things, had made the Royal family "relatable." The cat, and Erin, with her natural athletic grace, her easy way, her intelligence, her charm, her instinct for how to do the right thing, had brought his family out of the Dark Ages.

She had done it so gently, and with such humor and compassion, that it had not been a painful transition.

It seemed the last flower had been laid, when the garden gate swung open. Milo came through it, though you could barely tell it was him for the size of the giant spray of yellow flowers he carried. He was weeping noisily as he walked. He knelt before the grave, set his flowers on it.

This is who Erin was. Hugely pregnant, she didn't even hesitate to get back on her knees. She knelt beside Milo, put her arm around him and leaned her head against his shaking shoulder.

She was putting away her own pain to bring him comfort.

The staff—Milo—were here for the cat, of course. But it was really for her, to acknowledge the gift she had brought to this island and to his household. Humanity.

These people were not her staff.

They were the family she had always wanted. And they knew it.

Valentino knew it. He was her family. Soon,

they would welcome a baby. Despite pressure to reveal the sex, the truth was they lived by their motto—*to surprises*—and did not themselves know whether the child would be a boy or a girl.

He looked at the two people kneeling by the small grave. This was life then: one day you said hello and one day you said goodbye.

He could feel them rising to the challenge, dancing with the timeless, glorious, endless cycle of death and birth.

And love. That incredible force that Valentino had come to know.

That power that transcended it all.

* * * * *

If you enjoyed this story,
check out these other great reads from
Cara Colter

The Wedding Planner's Christmas Wish
His Cinderella Next Door
Matchmaker and the Manhattan Millionaire
One Night with Her Brooding Bodyguard

All available now!